DOUBLE DOG DARE

ELLEN RIGGS

BOUGHT-THE-FARM
MYSTERIES

Free Fun Story!

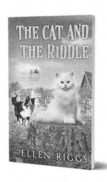

Can this sleuthing sheepdog solve a riddle in time to save a missing cat?

Ivy, Edna, Gertie team up with Keats and Percy to outwit a wily catnapper in this Bought-the-Farm story. Join Ellen Riggs' author newsletter today at **ellen-riggs.com** to receive *The Cat and the Riddle* FREE.

Double Dog Dare

Copyright © 2022 Ellen Riggs

ISBN 978-1-990613-07-4 eBook
ISBN 978-1-990613-06-7 Book
ASIN B09XYL6Y6K Kindle
ASIN TBD Paperback
Publisher: Ellen Riggs

www.ellenriggs.com
Cover designer: Lou Harper
Editor: Serena Clarke
2208161804

CHAPTER ONE

The bright, crisp morning was meant for shoveling manure. Out behind the barn, I finished my third coffee, put on my work gloves and got ready to immerse myself, figuratively speaking. This great pile of fertilizer had long been my favorite place on Runaway Farm. Recently, it became the site of the most romantic moment of my life and inspired me to spend even more time creating wonder out of waste.

It was honorable work and I didn't particularly care if others agreed. There was no pleasing some people, including my furry best friends.

A certain sheepdog with a penchant for perpetual motion was in a huff. His ears were flat, his tail down and his muzzle directed resolutely away. He withheld the warmth of his brown eye yet allowed the blue one to turn back occasionally and pierce me with a chilling glare.

Keats was bored, but it was about more than that. Hours ago, I'd offended him deeply and he couldn't forgive. The dog with the huge heart—the one who would literally die for me—also knew how to hold a grudge.

"Just let it go, buddy," I said. "Don't blame me for the weather."

When I rolled out of bed at five a.m., the frosty tip of my nose confirmed that autumn had passed and winter begun. That meant it was coat season. The dog abhorred wearing a jacket, whereas Percy, my ginger cat, adored his yellow bomber.

Our morning chores had taken ages because Keats periodically collapsed under the weight of his pride. I allowed him to indulge his feelings until he nearly let Drama Llama slip past him and out of the pasture. My latest showdown with the cranky camelid was still very fresh in my mind and I didn't care for another. A sharp reprimand unsettled the dog further and now he wasn't speaking to me at all. We'd gone a full hour with nary a mumble, let alone a pant-laugh. My mind felt strangely empty, and I realized how often it was full of mostly unspoken conversation with my black-and-white companion. We'd become so interconnected that I barely had a thought to call my own. I blamed that on the concussion I'd sustained while rescuing my pup. Sometimes it felt like a driven border collie was behind my mental curtain running the show.

At any rate, this discord was ruining my manure high. I needed to make amends while still being a responsible owner who kept her pets warm. If I folded on the coat, it would be a slippery slope into barnyard chaos.

Turning away from the pile, I tossed the dog a grin. "Let's go on an adventure, Keats. Have some fun."

The blue eye turned again, letting me know that fun was dead and buried till spring arrived and coats came off for good. This was the season of his discontent.

"Oh, come on. Thanksgiving is just around the corner. We'll have guests at the inn right through the holidays. It's going to be awesome."

He allowed a mumble, but only to disagree with me. "Awesome" was banned from our joint lexicon till spring, too. Furthermore, his tone suggested that life had been unspeakably dull in the weeks since we exposed an exotic pet ring. I was failing him in every way that counted.

"That bad, huh? It's super tough to be you right now, obviously."

There was more canine backtalk about the deplorable conditions. This hobby farmer needed to pull up her overall straps and provide a quality experience for an exemplary sheepdog.

"If we go for a drive, we might sniff out a mystery," I said. "It happens."

An insolent grumble suggested he was out on a sleuthing strike, too.

That was a load of manure and I knew it. Keats would never pass up a mystery as long as a heart beat under that little black jacket.

Percy meowed down at me from the roof of the barn. He liked to hang out up there to survey his domain and get a jump on trouble. Literally.

"You're right, my feline friend." I shielded my eyes from the sun. Percy was always hard to miss with his orange fluff, but the neon yellow coat turned him into a beacon. "We need to find this dog a mystery. Let's see where the road takes us."

Keats' ears perked up but he lagged behind as I walked through the barn and out the other side. Percy shot down from the roof like a brilliant comet and landed on the hood of my truck. I expected it but still jumped and gasped. Finally, the dog produced a single "ha." If seeing me nonplussed lifted his spirits, I was willing to take the hit for the team.

I let the pets in through the driver's door and then slid behind the wheel. "Where to, Keats? This is your pity party."

All that got me was another frosty blue stare. The time for

jokes had not yet arrived.

"Look, I have a to-do list a mile long and Jilly's got another for me. Driving you around when we're holiday planning is probably going to get me in trouble."

Indeed, as I pulled the truck around, I saw my best friend running down the front stairs with her coat under her arm. Opening my window, I prepared for a barrage of requests. It had been a while since we had guests and we were a little rusty in the hospitality department. Jilly basically ran the inn with my sister, Daisy, and did all the cooking, too. She asked very little of me, but there was only so much of her to go around.

"Ivy, wait! Wherever you're going, I'm coming." She circled the truck and shooed the pets out of the passenger seat so that she could get in. "I can't take it anymore."

"Can't take *what* anymore? Cooking?"

She gave me a glare with green eyes nearly as bright and sharp as Percy's. "I'll never get tired of cooking, but I can't seem to get the kitchen to myself for a single second. Imagine that crowd on your manure pile and you'll understand."

The crowd in question consisted of my mother and my brother Asher, who was Jilly's husband of about a month.

"In this case, three really is a crowd," I said. "You've done the right thing by leaving."

She cracked open the window and sucked in fresh air. "I'm sorry. I know they're your family."

Heading down the lane, I smiled. "I'm well aware of their idiosyncrasies. Should we call a family meeting?"

I hoped Jilly didn't regret her decision either to marry Asher or continue living at the inn. She'd handled Mom easily before that, but now there were growing pains. Dahlia Galloway had a big personality. It took up two rooms at the inn and was making inroads on a third. She had no business encroaching on Jilly's culinary refuge.

"No, of course not." Jilly pulled her nose inside and the energy shifted. "It'll be fine when Asher goes back to work. He's wandering around trying to help where it's not needed and then Dahlia deliberately gets in his way. They're bickering."

"Let's give them a chance to sort it out while we're gone, but I have no problem sending Mom to her apartment in town. My best friend's peace of mind trumps family."

"I'm sure Kellan meant well by leaving Asher off the roster, but cops aren't good with downtime."

I wasn't convinced Kellan Harper, the police chief and my new fiancé, had my brother's best interests in mind at all. Asher roved around house and barn like a restless security guard. If he wasn't in Jilly's way, he was in mine. Like it or not, we'd acquired a personal police detail and neither man would admit it.

Turning out of the lane onto the highway, I followed subtle signs from the dog, who'd insinuated himself into Jilly's lap. Percy was on the back of her seat, planning his descent, too. "How'd you shake Asher?"

"He went into the bathroom and your mom started yammering at him through the door about setting up a shower schedule. Despite having four other available showers. That got him steamed up, and it was easy for me to bolt."

"Bet they don't notice you're gone for ages," I said. "There's been a turf war coming and they might as well blow the place up without us."

"Meanwhile, we're doing what, exactly?"

I waggled my eyebrows at her. "Looking for trouble."

"We need to look for it? Seems to find us all the time."

"Keats was bored and sulky about his coat. I had to do something." I talked over his indignant mumble. "You could probably use more mystery in your life, too, my friend. It's been a little quiet lately."

I expected her to deny it, but instead she shrugged. "If only we could choose our diversions. Guess that's too much to ask."

"Probably. Today, let's just play 'hunt the preppers.' I called Edna and Gertie and neither answered. That means they're up to no good, which is bound to be the distraction we need."

Keats gave a full-on happy pant. He liked where this was going.

Jilly's expression was less enthused. "What if they're refurbishing a bunker? Getting trapped in a dirt hole isn't my idea of an escape."

The dog stuck his muzzle out the open window and then directed me to turn off at the feed store. "They must be out in the bush," I said, heading for the entrance to the back country trail system. "Doing target practice or something."

"I hope they're not with the survivalist class," Jilly said. "We could end up as targets."

"Edna said she disbanded SurvivalDare because the students were so high maintenance. Her exact words were, 'Let the zombies take out the trash.'"

Jilly laughed for the first time and patted Keats' jacket lightly. "Where are they, buddy?"

The dog led us through so many bumpy, serpentine trails I wondered if he was deliberately getting me lost to punish me for the coat infraction. It wasn't like him to be vindictive, though, and he had a very soft spot for Jilly, who was gripping the doorhandle for dear life.

"We're getting close," I said, trying to tune into whatever Keats was mumbling out the window. His tail bristled slightly, and I had no doubt that his hackles were rising under the coat. Percy answered the dog with a low growl, orange tail lashing.

"Close to what?" Jilly asked.

I rounded the last turn. "Close to something that might make us wish we were bored again."

CHAPTER TWO

J illy sat up straight and released the handle. "What on earth are they doing?"

The answer wasn't clear even after we jumped out of the truck to join our octogenarian friends, Edna Evans and Gertie Rhodes. They were pacing back and forth across a wide clearing, ignoring us completely.

As usual, Gertie was wearing her baggy brown poncho, with her long, heavy braid hanging down her back. In the time I'd known her, it had grown past her buttocks and must surely be a whiplash hazard. Wrangling her rifle, Minnie, around the poncho seemed like challenge enough.

Edna was also in her usual garb, specifically, fatigues and combat boots. Her helmet and gloves lay off to one side with her huge backpack. She didn't look up as we came over, so intent was she on her task. Each bare hand clasped one prong of a forked stick, while the long end stuck straight out ahead of her as she walked slowly over the dry grass.

"If you have to ask, I'm not answering, Ivy," she said, before I could open my mouth. "You'd know this if you'd taken my class."

"We got turned down for your class, remember?"

"I would have let you in if you'd pushed harder." She lifted her eyes long enough to give us a scornful look. "You two want to rely on your handsome men when the end comes. That's a big mistake."

"Don't diss our men," Jilly said. "They're amazing."

"Debatable," Edna said. "My point was more that *you're* amazing. You don't need to follow their lead when you could be leading them. And others."

Gertie flicked Minnie over her shoulder and grinned. "We need more female warriors. Men get so sidetracked by ego and competition. Even my Saul, bless his heart."

"Is this a warrior task?" Jilly asked. "Edna's carrying a stick around with perfect posture. Will there be beauty pageants or camo fashion shows after the apocalypse?"

Edna's scorn intensified. "Oh, Jillian. You've gone downhill since your nuptials, as I predicted. This activity should be perfectly obvious."

"I know what you're doing," I said. "Dowsing. What I want to know is why. And also, *why here?*"

Jilly bent to scoop up Percy. "Dowsing? You mean that stick is a divining rod?"

"Ding-ding-ding. Good guess." Edna started walking again. "This site could host a future encampment if there's underground water. We won't be able to count on streams after the end times. They'll be full of toxins."

I pointed at her dowsing rod. "It's bobbing. Does that mean there's water?"

"There's something underfoot, but like I was telling Gertie before you descended on us uninvited, it doesn't feel like water. Dowsing can also detect other things."

"Like what?" I asked.

"Metal, for starters. I've found some old relics out here. Sold them for a good price, too."

"To the Langman sisters?" Jilly said. "I thought we were boycotting their store."

Gertie spoke for Edna. "We'd never share our spoils with those shameless vultures. Besides, they prefer bilking grieving families out of regular antiques."

"There were plenty of reputable vendors willing to take gold coins off our hands," Edna said. "Built up my disaster fund nicely."

Jilly looked decidedly more interested. "You're saying this forked stick helped you find buried gold?"

"Sure," Gertie said. "And the metal detector confirmed it."

My curiosity was piqued. "What else have you found?"

"Not as much as we should have, given the time we've spent," Gertie said. "But now I understand why so many people used to trespass on my property searching for treasure. It's more addictive than bingo. Just when you're about to quit, your number comes up."

"Dopamine," Jilly said. She rocked the cat, who still hadn't relaxed. "Plus serotonin and adrenaline. Someone needs to start a twelve-step program for hill country treasure hunters."

Edna did a few short turns and the stick bobbed at the same points in her journey each time. "We've got a hit, but it's hard to know whether it's worth the effort of digging. Especially when the ground's nearly frozen. This is why I want to try ground-penetrating radar. I prefer traditional methods, but there's a time and place for technology."

"Especially for two old dames like us," Gertie said. "We don't have decades to unearth hill country's secrets."

"Speak for yourself," Edna said. "I feel confident enough in our longevity to invest in the right tools."

I gestured for her to turn. "You don't need fancy technology,

Edna. My dog's saying you're a couple of feet off the mark. He could save you some digging."

Keats' white front paw was raised in a point and every trace of boredom had left his demeanor. I might have smiled if his ears and tail weren't broadcasting trouble.

"I'm going to hazard a guess it's not gold coins today," Jilly said, as the cat squirmed to get down.

Percy trotted briskly over in his garish bomber and circled the dog. Then he lifted one orange paw and gazed around our group to make sure he had our undivided attention.

He did. When Percy moved like that, he always got our attention.

The fluffy paw scraped an elaborate arc across the dirt nearly a foot away from Keats. Turned out the dog had been a little off, too.

"Uh-oh," I said, as the cat continued to deploy his litter box maneuver. "Jilly's right. Not coins. Unless someone was buried with a pocketful of change."

Crossing her arms, Jilly winced. "Maybe this time Percy's wrong. You know he scrapes randomly sometimes. Like around Justine Schalow."

He did indeed treat the reporter from the Clover Grove Tattler as nothing more than litter box waste, when she remained very much alive and a thorn in my side. I hadn't forgiven her for dumping her cheery little monk parrot on me, although the bird was now living the good life with Hester Weddle and her African gray.

"There's only one way to find out," Edna said. "Grab my spade, Ivy."

Instead, I knelt beside my pets and parted matted weeds with my gloved hands. Sunk into the ground were two nine-inch strips of old wood, tied with a disintegrating leather cord.

"It's a cross," I said, as everyone leaned over me. "Probably a grave marker."

The furry half of the dowsing team moved away and repeated the show, with a point and a scrape. Gertie followed the pets. She stooped over, groaning as the butt of the rifle clunked against her head. "Another cross."

Standing, I brushed soil from my overalls and looked at Jilly. "How's that for a distraction?"

"Not exactly what I had in mind," she said. "Finding old coins would have been fun. Old bones, less so."

Gertie started to speak, cleared her throat, and tried again. "How about *new* ones, then?"

CHAPTER THREE

I turned quickly and saw my pets had moved to the edge of the bush, which was dark and vaguely menacing despite the early hour. Keats pointed to a mound of rocky soil concealed rather obviously with branches and Percy climbed aboard to confirm the verdict with gusto.

Judging by the smell of fresh earth, the resident underneath was a newcomer to a neighborhood no one ever left.

Edna walked over and inspected the probable gravesite. "Look at those rocks. Eons ago, this used to be a lake bed."

"And now it's an eternal resting place for three deadbeats," Gertie said. "If not more."

"How do you know they're deadbeats?" Jilly asked, pulling out her phone. "They could be pets for all we know."

Straightening, Edna grimaced. "According to my dowsing rod, the first 'pet' was about six feet tall and bipedal. Are you aware of any animal matching that description, Jillian?"

My best friend tapped out a number and shrugged. "Sasquatch?"

"They're much taller from what I've heard," Edna said. "And unlikely to bother with a cross."

Gertie adjusted her rifle and looked around. "Regular folk probably wouldn't bury family out here. If they did, they'd use a proper grave marker."

"I assume we're standing among departed members of the criminal underworld," Edna said. "Probably never reported nor missed."

"Kellan has a big pile of files like that." I lowered my voice because Jilly was talking to the police now. "Unsolved crimes, mostly historical. I can understand the first two, but the fresh grave doesn't make sense. Why would anyone add a new body to an old burial site? How would they even know it existed?"

"Deadbeats have a grapevine, too," Gertie said. "Works even better than ours."

Edna crossed to her backpack and grabbed a spade. "Let's take a little poke around."

"Let's not," Jilly said, looking up from her phone. "It's a crime scene. You know the drill. No drilling."

"Just the old graves," Edna said. "My long nursing career revealed enough horrors without checking out the recent deposit. Mind you, I'd guess from the soil that the last one went into the body bank within days."

I held up my hand to stop her. "Old crime still counts. The police will want to start from scratch."

"What happened to your spirit of adventure, Ivy?" Edna said, smirking. "Oh, right, you've given up your renegade status and prematurely assumed the title of Mrs. Chief Hottie."

"I'm sure Kellan hopes I'll give up my renegade status, but it'll never happen unless or until there's a baby on board. Besides, we haven't even set a wedding date."

"Like that ever stopped anyone," Gertie said, smirking too. "Saul and I—"

"Gertie, the police don't need to hear the spicy details," Jilly said, pressing the phone to her chest. "Not that we're judging."

Edna dropped her spade with a deliberate clatter. "I've always considered it dreadfully unfair that women have a best-before date while older men get to—"

"Ladies." Jilly's voice had an edge now. "Let me finish this call. Please."

I turned my back on her and lowered my voice. "Edna, you can stop worrying. I'm never going to quit the band, even if there are little Chief Hotties. Keats and Percy wouldn't stand for it. Our work can evolve."

Jilly's voice rose. I could tell Bunhead Betty was at the other end from the number of times my friend had to repeat herself. The police receptionist was far from stupid, but Betty's contempt for us and our activities often meant we had to jump through hoops simply to report a crime. It was easier to solve it ourselves than deal with the gatekeeper.

Percy sporadically swept his claws over the newest grave. Normally he stopped after a few minutes and I wondered if his persistence pointed to a bigger problem than usual. Mind you, three graves *was* a bigger problem than usual. Bigger than I cared to tackle without police backing. The old crimes were more work but the new ones were more risky. There was no winning.

There was also no boredom.

Looking to Keats for answers, I was surprised to see him heading into the bush. His tail was at half-mast. There was something to see in there, but it likely wasn't the killer.

Percy had his own opinion. His paw stopped moving and his brilliant eyes narrowed to slits as he looked in the direction Keats had gone. Then he gave a loud hiss and shot after the dog.

"Weird," I said. "Hissing isn't usually part of Percy's grave-side etiquette. I'm going to see what the fuss is about."

Jilly finished her call and dropped the phone back in her

purse. "Not alone, you aren't. I'll come with you while we wait for the police."

"Maybe someone armed would be the better candidate," Edna said.

I glanced back as we headed for the bush. "Maybe someone armed with a dowsing rod could do a full headcount and have bragging rights with the police."

"Like I care about such things." Edna scoffed, but she also turned back to the graves. "On the other hand, if I rack up enough points, Chief Fiancé might give me back my license."

"It's only right," Gertie said. "You're one heck of a driver, old friend."

Inclining her permed head modestly, Edna accepted the praise. "One day Kellan will accept my challenge to a drag race and I'll hand him his chiefly ego on a platter."

Searching for the entrance to the trail the pets had taken, I called, "Chief Fiancé deserves some respect, Edna."

Her tart retort was swallowed by foliage. The boys were so far ahead that I began feeling uneasy. Come to think of it, I'd felt uneasy from the moment we left the truck. My own hackles had prickled a vague warning I'd ignored. Initially, I felt we were being watched but Keats had been caught up in dowsing for bodies. He hadn't signaled a significant threat, so I wondered if my unconscious mind was on overdrive. These days, I found myself in a chronic state of hypervigilance. There was too little time between crimes to regulate my nervous system with benign tasks, like building fences, dancing with an alpaca or turning manure.

Jilly's voice from behind startled me out of my thoughts. "I haven't felt right since we got out of the truck. It's like someone has been watching us the whole time."

My instincts weren't just hypervigilance, after all. "Same.

Justine is my first guess. Hasn't tailed me in a week. I hoped she'd found someone else to torment."

"I saw her outside the library yesterday," Jilly said. "Dottie Bridges was giving her a good dressing down over some infraction."

"Why didn't you tell me earlier? I would have sent Dottie flowers and a thank you card."

The town's librarian hadn't always been my hero but it was one of many relationships that had surprised me with its growth.

She laughed. "I was saving it for the right moment."

"This is the right moment? While we're potentially tailing a killer?"

"I doubt the killer's out here. Keats didn't seem too upset about it."

"Percy did, though. How often does your cat-baby hiss?"

She thought about that. "Rarely. Normally the boys agree on the level of alert. Today Keats is at amber and Percy red. Maybe we should go back and wait for the police."

A sharp yip ahead told us to get a move on it.

"Sounds like it's a little late for that." I thrashed harder at the bushes to speed our progress. "We're nearly there. Wherever 'there' is."

A startled screech rang out. I recognized the exact pitch. A woman had just experienced a sheepdog nip.

"Keats got her good," I said. "Justine's legs are going to be permanently scarred at the rate she's going."

But the legs disappearing up a tree as we broke through the wall of shrubs and entered a clearing didn't belong to Justine Schalow.

CHAPTER FOUR

The reporter who typically dogged me had a scrawny frame concealed by baggy clothes, whereas the woman clambering up the tree had more meat on her bones.

Not that this was the time to be pondering any bones but those of the deceased back in the clearing.

The stranger was wearing what appeared to be nice jeans, now with a couple of fang marks, and smart boots that were better suited to window-shopping than hard climbing. By this point she was high enough that I couldn't see more detail. Her ragged breathing said it was a tough slog, but I gave her points for persisting.

A pant-laugh told me Keats was well satisfied. So much so that he seemed to have forgotten his depression over the winter coat. His blue eye quickly shot a frosty bullet into that idea and his canine laughter stopped.

Coming up behind him, I stared at his treed victim. "Afraid of dogs? I'd like to say he doesn't bite but of course you know better."

The woman looking down at us was probably in her mid-twenties. Her long hair wasn't far off the shade of Percy's tawny underparts. I could make the comparison because he was standing on the limb below her.

"I'm not afraid of dogs," she said. "Far from it. The cat's the one I'm worried about. He went after my fanny like a cougar."

Jilly and I both snickered. Butt-biting wasn't a signature move for Percy. "Sorry," I said. "He must have had his reasons. The first being that you were spying on us."

"We were not spying," she said, wrapping both arms around the trunk. I could see her white knuckles from 10 feet below. "We were just watching."

"Watching, spying... Sounds identical in my books. And who's 'we'?"

She tipped her head gently to the left. Far out on a nearly bare limb sat a gray cat with stunning green eyes. Delicate features told me the feline was female.

"Meet Fanny," she said. "I'm Louisa May Gentry."

Her blue eyes gazed at me expectantly, as if she thought I'd know the name. I couldn't recall anyone with that surname in Clover Grove, but my history was far from complete. One day, after the memory of what happened with the rabbits receded, I'd spend some quality time in the cemetery meeting the locals. If stumbling on old graves was going to become a regular happening, it would pay to get a who's who.

"I'm Ivy Galloway and this is Jilly Blackwood." I turned to my best friend. "Still using Blackwood?"

"Today," she said, with a little grin. "We'll see how it goes."

I looked back at Louisa May. "I'm assuming you know who we are and aren't just stalking random farmers and innkeepers."

Her blue eyes narrowed and her cheeks flushed. "It's not stalking when you came for the express purpose of introducing yourself."

"You took a roundabout way of doing that. Especially if you tailed us from my farm, which I can only assume you did."

She tried to shrug, nearly lost her grip, and thought better of it. "It's not tailing if you're just trying to catch up with someone. You drive like a maniac."

"You caught up with me. Ergo, you drive like a maniac, too."

"And it cost me my car, which overheated. I covered the last bit on foot."

"Guess it also cost you some jeans," I added. "Maybe even the boots. The bill for spying is racking up fast."

Her sniff was still cocky. "As long as I keep control of my bodily functions. When I saw what you found out there it was touch and go. I decided to change back to plan A."

"Which was...?"

A sigh drifted down to us. "Knocking on your front door. Like a normal person."

I fought a smile. There was something appealing about her spunk under pressure, and Keats' rising tail agreed.

"And are you?" Jilly asked. "A normal person?"

Adjusting her grip on the tree, our captive shook her head once. "I suppose not. Some say I'm 'different,' and I doubt they mean it as a compliment."

Now I really did smile. "Normal is overrated. Jilly and I like different, as long as we're not getting ambushed."

"It's not an ambush when you're the one up the tree."

"Sure, it is," Jilly said. "Just a failed one."

"You've got a lot of excuses, Louisa May," I said. "You sound like me."

Jilly laughed. "She does. You rationalize like that all the time, Ivy."

"I know," Louisa May said. "I did my research."

That ended the merriment. I didn't like it when people were reading up on me. Not only was it an invasion of my privacy, it also curtailed my movements. "Are you a reporter? If so, you'd better make yourself comfortable for a long stay. Or risk falling."

"She's conveniently located near the gangster graveyard," Jilly said. "We could drag her there pretty easily and let the cops process another one."

"The newspaper coverage didn't do justice to your wit," our captive said. "At least, I assume you're joking."

"About the graveyard, yes. About keeping you up there till you spill your story, no."

She scanned around, as if assessing her chances of any other escape. Without wings, they were slim to none. "Call off your cat, please. I'm willing to risk myself but not Fanny. She's the best cat in the world."

"Impossible, since I already own the best cat in the world." I glanced at Jilly. "Or we do. We share him."

"Percy, come down please," Jilly said. "This day is turning into a doozy, and I need you."

He fired off a last hiss, not at Louisa, but Fanny. So that's why his tail was in a knot earlier. The presence of another cat had riled him. It was strange, because he had gotten along well with over 100 cats in a feral colony, and never took issue with our current barn cats. There must be more to pretty Fanny than met the eye.

Once Jilly's arms were full of marmalade fluff, I looked up again and raised my eyebrows. "Well? You've worked hard for this moment. What do you want?"

"It's not what I want, but my aunt. Maud Gentry." Again she looked at me expectantly. "Does the name ring a bell?"

I shook my head. "Should it?"

"I would hope so." She unfurled the fingers of one hand long enough to point down at Keats. "Because you have her dog."

CHAPTER FIVE

Fluffy black ears immediately arrived under my fingertips to provide support. "I have her—*what*?"

"You heard me. My aunt breeds border collies and Keats was stolen from her at a dog show nearly two years ago. Of course, he wasn't called Keats, then."

Jilly squeezed my arm and spoke for me. "What was he called?"

"Yeats," Louisa said. "Same dog, different poet. Isn't that a strange coincidence?"

"Very. But you can't prove this is the same dog," Jilly said. "We've seen dozens of border collies with one blue eye."

Dozens was stretching it, but the herding trials we'd attended had turned up a few lesser specimens of my gorgeous sheepdog. Some had his fine tuxedo and white-tipped tail, too.

"I don't need to prove it's the same dog," Louisa said. "He already did. His ears twitched when I said his name."

Jilly shrugged. "His ears twitch all the time. And if he knew you, he wouldn't have nipped your leg and chased you up a tree."

"He would if he felt I was a threat to Ivy. He's bonded with his captor. What do they call that? Stockholm syndrome?"

"I did not steal this dog," I blurted.

"It was all over the papers," Louisa said. "On TV, too. You bragged about it."

"I was concussed. More importantly, I stole him from a murderer, not from your aunt. How was I to know his original owner?"

"The microchip?" Louisa had gained enough confidence to flutter her fingers around. That attitude could come back to bite her hard in the fanny.

I started to cross my arms and then decided to leave one hand on Keats. What I really wanted to do was pick him up and run before she could try to reclaim him on her aunt's behalf. Unfortunately, she knew exactly where I lived.

Keats wouldn't join her without a fight, however. Of that, I was sure.

He gave a mumble of agreement that sounded like, "Finders, keepers."

Jilly squeezed my arm harder. My brain seemed to be inflating in my skull like a helium balloon and there was a risk of an explosion that would leave quite a mess.

"There was no microchip," I said. "Several different vets confirmed that. If I'd been able to return him after I rescued him, I would have." I met Louisa's blue eyes more calmly. "I won't now."

My best friend released the squirming cat and took over again. "Your aunt will need to settle for money. I presume that's why you're here. To extort Ivy."

Louisa started to rear back, then remembered where she was and clutched the tree again with her free hand. Fanny stepped lightly along the bough and rubbed her head gently against her owner's chin. This stranger couldn't be all bad if there was so much love between them.

"I'm not here to reclaim the dog," she said. "Although my aunt would certainly like to breed him. I don't need to tell you he's a remarkable example of a border collie. That's why she started showing him early. He was supposed to be the lynchpin of her program."

Keats gave a bashful—or abashed—mumble. "He's neutered," I said. "There won't be any baby Keats, as much as I'd welcome them."

There was a horrified gasp overhead. "You don't neuter a dog with his lineage."

"I didn't know his lineage. Clearly. But I have enough animals to worry about without puppies underfoot. So, I suppose your aunt will want money for damages against lost income, too."

She shook her head again and her smart boots slid around enough to make her squeal. "My aunt doesn't want your money. Really."

Keats gave an exasperated mumble that told her to get to the point. When she didn't take his cue, I said it for him. "If your aunt doesn't want my dog or my money, what *does* she want?"

"Your help. *His* help." There was a quaver in her voice now. "She's in trouble."

CHAPTER SIX

K ellan and a small army of uniformed cops had gathered by the time we got back to the gangster graveyard. It took ages to coax Louisa and Fanny down from the tree and I didn't exactly blame them since I was no great fan of heights.

She refused to say another word about her aunt's plight from her precarious position and I didn't blame her for that, either. Now that I knew she wasn't trying to steal my dog, at least overtly, there was time to tease the story out of her.

Once her boots touched down, Keats got her moving briskly, and ran interference between Percy, who continued to be irascible, and Fanny, who climbed onto her owner's shoulder. Eventually, I scooped up my cat and we walked into the large clearing side by side, each with a cat in the pirate's parrot position.

My brother was back on duty—or at least halfway, with his uniform shirt buttoned all wrong over faded jeans. He raced over to hug Jilly as if they'd been parted for years. He didn't care what his colleagues thought about his continued doting over his fair bride. The fact that she'd slipped away from the house while he was squabbling with Mom only seemed to make him fonder. If he thought bickering had driven her into another crime scene, however, he was wrong. Jilly was always behind the wheel of her own life.

Kellan came over, too, settling for touching my shoulder. Even that simple gesture was notable progress over his usual crime scene greeting. That may have been because the body in question was already buried, but I hoped it was a fiancé upgrade. By the time we were married, I might get a one-armed squeeze. Then, perhaps even a hug after becoming the mother of his children.

Except that I'd vowed not to be at crime scenes by then.

It was going to be a tough promise to keep because I didn't go looking for them. Well, technically, I had gone looking for a mystery today. But not a murder victim, let alone three. This was Edna's doing. You couldn't go dowsing in Clover Grove—or anywhere in hill country—without turning up problems.

I gazed up at Kellan for a moment, desperately wanting a hug but knowing it would embarrass him in front of his staff. He would think I was overcome by the discovery of these bodies, when I was actually just reeling from learning my beloved dog's previous owner was lurking in the shadows. What kind of trouble was Maud Gentry in? And why had she sent an emissary instead of coming herself? And the biggest question of all... if we agreed to help, were we walking into a trap?

Kellan stared from one cat to the other and blinked a few times. Then he offered his hand to Louisa. "I'm Chief Harper. Ivy's fiancé."

Heat rushed into my cheeks. His declaration was as good as a hug. Everyone else in the clearing already knew our status but hearing it out loud like that made it crime scene official.

Louisa touched Fanny, who delivered a head butt and a

fetching meow on cue. Up in the tree, our spy had looked bigger. Boots down, she was a little taller than Jilly and considerably shorter than me. Her attitude had shrunk, too. She shook Kellan's hand tentatively and deflated even more.

Jilly gave her a gentle shove. "This is Louisa May Gentry. She followed us out here, saying her aunt, Maud Gentry, is the previous owner of Keats. His breeder, in fact."

"Oh?" Kellan's dark blue eyes moved quickly to meet mine, although his expression otherwise stayed neutral. He'd always had the gift of hiding his feelings and it came in handy in his work. "And where is this aunt? Even if your claim is true, surely you didn't expect Ivy to surrender the dog."

Louisa found her voice at last. "My aunt is at home in Thistledown. She needs Ivy's help there."

Kellan spun his hand to speed her up. "Help with what, exactly?"

"She'd like to explain it herself," Louisa said. "My aunt's practically been in hiding since Yeats was stolen from the dog show."

"*Keats*," I said, touching the dog's ears again. "His name is Keats now. We prefer the romantic poets."

"Yeats," Kellan muttered. "That's odd."

It certainly was. I couldn't imagine how I'd come up with a name so similar, even if it was pronounced differently. When I discovered my pup in the criminal's yard, the name just popped into my mind.

"The whole thing is odd," Jilly said, evaluating our stalker with a critical eye. "How do we know your aunt won't ambush us like you just did?"

"Bring one of your cops if you're worried," Louisa said. "They can start by looking up my aunt. I assure you she has a clean record."

Kellan signaled Asher to do just that and my brother walked

away. "In the meantime, you can give us the details, Miss Gentry."

"Like I said, Chief, it's a private matter. My aunt will explain."

He shook his head. "You have two options. Give me the story or give me her number. As you've probably realized, we have a situation here that demands my attention. Please don't try my patience with your evasions."

I didn't often let my guy fight my battles, but when my dog's safety was potentially at risk, I was happy to lean back.

Our visitor shifted uneasily, and Fanny rocked with her, as if riding the good ship Louisa was a breeze. "Could we at least move away from the crowd?"

Glancing around, Kellan nodded. "I suppose. If it will speed your storytelling."

It did. When our circle narrowed to Louisa, Kellan, Jilly and me, the words spilled out. "My aunt not only lost Keats to thieves, but later his mother. There were so many break-ins that Maud moved to Thistledown, which is barely a town, as you probably know. Things seemed safe there until two days ago. We went to a family wedding and that's when it happened."

"That's when *what* happened?" Kellan pressed.

"Someone stole her most prized possession."

He spun his index finger again. "Jewelry? Antiques?"

Louisa shook her head hard enough to rock Fanny, who let out a yowl of complaint. "My aunt doesn't care about any of that. They stole Yeats' sister. From the dog-sitter's house." She directed a palm at me. "Keats. Whatever. I saw you on the news ages ago and realized it was our stolen dog. We know all about the work you've been doing. How gifted he is." Her voice got shaky. "And it seemed like you might be able to help us find her."

"Your own police should be doing that job." Kellan's voice

was gentler now. "It might not be safe for Ivy, and particularly Keats. Who's to say someone won't try to steal him again?"

My hand clamped down on Keats' ears but he didn't flinch. Instead, he mumbled a challenge. An "I'd like to see them try" sort of sound. The first time he was dognapped, he was barely out of puppyhood. Now he knew how to fight, and there was an army behind him.

"Chief Harper, you know we don't have a police force in Thistledown," Louisa said. "We share three cops with four small towns and a missing dog didn't even warrant a visit. As with Clover Grove, crime is on the rise there. They sent us to Animal Services. We're big enough to have a pound, small enough to be policing ourselves."

Kellan thought about this and nodded. "I know that's happening in many areas, and I'm sorry. As soon as I can spare an officer, I'll send someone down to help."

Louisa reached for his arm, but stopped short. "Chief, please. All we need is Ivy and Keats. And Jilly. And maybe those old ladies, if they'll come."

"Oh, we'll come," Edna said. She and Gertie had gradually inched close enough to eavesdrop. "Although if you call me an old lady again, it'll be the last time you need lipstick."

"Miss Evans," Kellan said. "That sounded too much like a threat for my liking."

"Chief, the only thing old here is a couple of graves," Edna said. "And you're just sore I won't be here to help you ID what my dowsing rod turned up."

"I don't believe in dowsing," Kellan said. "There's absolutely no science behind it."

"Yet here we are," Gertie said, sweeping the muzzle of her rifle toward the gangster graveyard. "Maybe we should stay back and give you a hand. This is too big a job for the cops alone."

Kellan rolled his eyes. At the same time, he brightened,

probably at the prospect of running his investigation unimpeded for a change. "Visiting Thistledown is okay with me if it's okay with Ivy," he said.

I nodded. "If Keats' sister is missing, it's our duty to help. But we won't come without Percy, Louisa."

She blanched and reached for her cat again. "That thing is feral. A savage. Fanny can't defend herself."

"You're underestimating her," I said. "Anyway, Percy is a critical part of my team. Take one, take all."

Fanny seemed to cast the deciding vote with a delicate mew. "Fine," Louisa said. "But you're covering any vet bills."

"We'll see," I said, handing Percy over to Jilly.

"And my car repairs, too," she said. "You burned out my engine."

"It was your boot on the gas pedal." I gave her a chilling stare worthy of Keats' blue eye. "Keep it up and you can hitch-hike home."

"We'll get your car towed, Ms. Gentry," Kellan said. "You'd never find your way out of here anyway."

"Let's deploy before the missing dog's trail gets stale," Edna said, pulling on her gloves.

"I'll contact my colleagues in the area and put them on notice." Kellan touched my shoulder again. "You'll let me know if you get a whiff of danger, right?"

"Absolutely." Mostly I waited till there was far more than a whiff, but being his fiancée meant I had to level up my game.

"I mean it, Ivy," he said.

"I know you do. And I mean it, too."

He leaned over and hugged me, without even looking to see if his staff were watching. Afterward, he turned to Jilly. "Guess I'll have some explaining to do with Officer Galloway for letting you go."

Jilly gave a rueful nod. "You sure will, Chief. I don't envy you that."

Keats mumbled some marching orders. Leaving my side for the first time, he started gathering the troops.

The nip he gave Louisa was entirely unnecessary but satisfying all the same. I bet she tasted no better than Justine.

CHAPTER SEVEN

Edna and Gertie had go-kits at the ready, so they showed
Louisa and Fanny around the farm while Jilly and I gathered our things inside. Keats went along to keep an eye on the
guests, his posture neutral but his movements wary.

Percy, meanwhile, followed us from room to room wailing at
every window.

"What is your problem, Percy?" I asked. "Fanny seems
sweet. The nicer of the two, actually. You'll need to travel in
your crate until you get that mood in check."

Louisa and Fanny had caught a ride to the farm with Gertie
for the cat's safety, but I wanted them to drive with Jilly and me
to Thistledown. An hour on the road would help us pull more
information out of Louisa and prepare us better for what we
might encounter on this strange—and hopefully short
—adventure.

We packed for a couple of days, just in case. Maybe we'd get
lucky and find the missing dog right away, but things were rarely
that simple. We could stay in a motel near Thistledown if
needed. No way would I sleep under Maud Gentry's roof. No

matter what Louisa said, her aunt probably had designs on Keats.

"I'm surprised you'd let Louisa nose around the farm," Jilly said, as we met at the top of the stairs with our backpacks. "Do you trust her?"

"Nope. Nor her aunt. There's something fishy about this story. I mean, why would criminals target her dogs specifically? They were valuable to her as breeding stock, but even a border collie with a great pedigree isn't that pricy. Plus, there are easier ways to make a living than raising puppies."

"I'm not buying it either," Jilly said, leading me downstairs. She glanced longingly into her now-empty kitchen. Asher was back on the job and Mom had left, too. Just as our space freed up, we had to join a posse on the road. "This Louisa is awfully pushy for someone asking a big favor."

"I think the attitude's a front. She strikes me as insecure. No one's ever climbed a tree to evade us before."

Jilly put her pack down by the front door and sighed. "I used to give people the benefit of the doubt. Now I assume the worst unless proven wrong."

"Oh, please," I said, laughing. "We *always* assumed the worst. In Boston we turned cynicism into an art form. That's stood us in good stead here."

She laughed, too. "I guess. The truth will come out eventually. In the meantime, let's keep a close eye on the Gentry women and an even closer eye on Keats."

I peered out the window in the door. The dog was still in my sightline but I missed him. Sensing it, he turned and offered a play bow. "I shouldn't have made him wear his coat today. What if—"

"Ivy, don't even go there. They wouldn't dare make a play for him. And if they so much as look at him wrong, we'll put them in their place."

"What if he wants to stay?" The quaver in my voice was as noticeable as Louisa's had been earlier. "Did you think about that? He might miss his breeder. She must have something going for her to produce such a great dog."

"A great dog who's watching you now with all the love in the world in his eyes," she said, standing on tiptoe to look out at him. "No way will he stay with Maud Gentry or anyone else."

I nodded too hard and realized a migraine was lying in wait for me. It had been more than a month since the last one, which was a personal record. Stress brought them on, but not just any stress. My head didn't ache facing a murderer, but the prospect of losing my dog had definitely rattled some neurons.

"I wanted Louisa to see the farm so that she could vouch for the place to her aunt," I said, turning away from the door. "He has everything a sheepdog could want here. Room to run, plenty of livestock and—"

"Mysteries to solve?" Jilly interrupted with a sly grin.

"That might work against me. She could say I put him in harm's way."

"More like the other way around. What counts is that he has a loving home. And a community that values him highly, including the police. No matter what Maud Gentry has to offer, it can't equal the life he has here."

"I never thought twice about neutering him," I said. "It was just the thing you do, although there's so much conflicting information about it now."

Jilly pulled out her phone and started tapping. "Definitely the right decision. He can focus fully on the job at hand, rather than chasing girlfriends."

"Right? Keats' value goes far past siring puppies. He's contributed so much to public safety with his laser focus on solving crime."

She looked up from her phone to give me her full attention.

"We need to laser focus on the job at hand, too. There's no point regretting or speculating. He's your dog. You're a team. A fabulous partnership."

I dropped my eyes to the backpacks at our feet, knowing the discussion could have a teary conclusion. "I doubt he would work for anyone else. Even his breeder."

"He told you so. I heard that mumble. His loyalty is a till-death-do-you-part commitment. If they pulled any funny business, he'd spend the rest of his days trying to get back here."

A couple of tears ran down my cheeks. "They'll have to fight me. I'm stronger than I used to be and have lots of support. Including the best friend in the world."

"And an influential fiancé." Her smile came out from behind the clouds. "Have you gotten used to that word yet?"

It was a welcome distraction and I jumped on it. "No, and I probably won't until it's time to use the word husband."

"An even bigger hurdle," she said, going back to typing her notes. "Are you going to change your name?"

Bending, I opened the door of the cat carrier and Percy stepped inside. "Probably not. Until we moved here, I wasn't at all attached to the family name. Now, despite all their antics, I'm glad to be a Galloway. If it's important to Kellan, I could hyphenate."

"I doubt he'll care. Asher, on the other hand, has been pressuring me."

"Doesn't surprise me anymore." Hoisting my pack, I opened the door, and then lifted the cat carrier. "He's way more traditional than I ever knew. Blackwood-Galloway could work, no?"

"Bit of a mouthful." She dropped her phone back in her purse, grabbed her pack and closed the door behind us. "I'll just keep dancing around it as long as I can."

We walked down the front steps together. "Till the first kid arrives, you mean."

"Sounds about right."

I slid Percy's crate into the back seat and then loaded our packs into the bed of the truck. "I figured things would get less complicated once we got the romance part sorted out."

"It's presented a different set of challenges." She waggled her left hand at me. "Along with lots of rewards, including pretty baubles."

I flashed my left hand at her quickly—but not quickly enough.

"Ivy Rose Galloway! What is on your ring finger?"

"Two beautiful engagement rings," I said. "And a black rubber washer from a faucet to hold them in place."

"They don't fit? You've been wearing them for three weeks."

"I think it's the cold weather. My fingers shrunk."

She stared at me incredulously. "Your brain has shrunk, and I mean that in the kindest possible way."

"There's nothing kind about telling a concussed woman her brain is withering." I was trying to throw her off the trail but that never worked. "I don't want to lose them, that's all."

"Which is the whole point of getting them fitted," she said. "They could end up in your manure pile."

"I wear gloves when I work, along with the washer."

I had shocked my friend dozens of times over the past year or two but this seemed to rock her to the core. Still, her expression grew milder. "This is a big deal, my friend. What's going on?"

Toying with the rings, I sighed. "I don't want to take them off even to be fitted. It's bad luck."

"You've never been particularly superstitious before."

"I never had a dog who can read my mind or a cat who predicts death, either. I guess I'm not as logical as I was in the corporate world."

She nodded, still trying to wrap her head around my fears.

"I hear you, but losing your rings would be terrible luck, right? What does Kellan say?"

"He doesn't know," I admitted. "I take off the rubber washer when he's around. His feelings might be hurt if he knew they didn't fit."

"Aha. This sounds like a Cinderella problem."

I couldn't help laughing as I stuck out one work boot. "Maybe."

"Well, let's get to the bottom of it right now."

Leaning against the truck, I stared up at the house. "I guess I can't quite believe Kellan proposed. Maybe I worry taking them off would give him a window to realize his mistake. That he got the wrong girl."

"That's never going to happen. Kellan knows his own mind. You don't get to be a police chief by waffling." She poked me with her ring finger and emeralds gleamed in the morning sun. "What's more, it's time for you to realize *you're* the real gem. That's what he thinks. Am I ever wrong about people?"

"There's a first time for everything."

"Not this time. If it helps, my rings are off a lot when I'm cooking and washing up. Asher hasn't changed his mind about me, has he?"

"Maybe it keeps him on his toes," I said. "And he sure loves his wedding ring. We never had anything nice, you know. I guess that's part of it." I angled my rings to catch the light. "Especially me, as the youngest. That's why I was always so frugal, even when I could afford some frills."

"I get that, because I never had much either. But I would be remiss as your best friend if I didn't caution you against fertilizing someone's future spuds with diamonds and garnets."

"I promise to get them fitted as soon as we're back," I told her, pushing off the truck.

"All the more reason to get going." She walked around to the passenger side. "Should I give Louisa the front seat?"

"Nah, she has to earn the prime real estate. Besides, Keats will want to be on your lap, and we need him calling the shots."

The others joined us, and we got Louisa settled in the rear with a crated cat on either side.

"I'm not big on the seating arrangements," she said, as both cats yowled.

"There's room with our backpacks," I said, jerking my thumb to the bed of the truck. "But you'll miss the scintillating conversation."

She crossed her arms and pouted. "I have nothing to say, anyway."

Jilly turned to her with a bright smile. "You could ride in Gertie's van. It's stuffed full of weapons but they'll squeeze you in."

"Don't worry about the bumps," I said. "Although there's always a risk of detonation."

Louisa stared straight ahead. "Hit it or quit it."

Keats echoed the sentiment and I led our little convoy down the lane.

CHAPTER EIGHT

Well before we reached Mandy's Country Store, I signaled and then turned into the lot.

"Why are we stopping?" Louisa asked. "Time is of the essence."

I parked the truck and glanced at her through the seats. "Pie is of the essence. That's how I start every investigation and I don't intend to change my strategy now, other than getting take-out. The only question is, two slices or three?"

"Two for me," Jilly said. "You know my favorites."

Louisa met my eyes, evaluating, and then said, "Three. And no rhubarb. Too close to a vegetable."

Keats gave a ha-ha-ha from Jilly's lap, knowing our guest had impressed me very much against my will.

"We'll stay here to keep it simple," Jilly said, knowing I wanted a private word with Mandy. "Louisa May and I can get to know each other."

"Just call me Lou," our passenger said. "If we're on a mission together, there's no need for formalities."

I reluctantly yielded her another point and opened the door, beckoning for Keats to join me.

Edna stuck her head out of the passenger window of Gertie's van. "Get a move on it, Ivy. There won't be pie after the apocalypse so you might as well start weaning yourself now."

I gave her a cheery wave. "We've talked about this. My apocalypse includes pie. Mandy will make it happen."

"Mandy McCain will never—"

My wave stopped and I directed my palm at Edna. "She will. And she's on team Ivy."

Edna persisted. "But she nearly got you—"

"Never mind. That was then, this is now."

Bickering with Edna nearly got me trampled by a man in jeans and a windbreaker who was coming down the stairs in a hurry.

"Oh, sorry," he said, with a bright smile that might have impressed a woman who wasn't affianced to someone with an even brighter one. "I almost kicked your dog."

Keats gave a mumble that turned into a low growl. My dog never got kicked because he was bred to avoid that very thing.

"We're good," I said, although Keats was much disgruntled. Either the comment or the guy's speed had rubbed him the wrong way. "I hope you tried the pie."

"Not this time," he said, with another flash of teeth. "But I'll be back. The coffee is great."

Something in his expression made me wonder if the purveyor of coffee had caught his interest, instead. If so, Mandy could do far worse. The man's eyes and hair were very dark and his skin quite pale, like a fairytale prince. The logo on his jacket said he could afford plenty of pie.

Keats circled to nudge me from behind, perhaps to remind me I was an engaged woman. I was grateful it wasn't a nip. Just because I was permanently off the market didn't mean I wanted to embarrass myself in front of a handsome man.

The next nudge had a hint of teeth that sent me hurtling

into the store. Mandy was behind the counter, looking as disgruntled as Keats.

"Was that guy hitting on you?" I asked, walking up to her with a smile.

"I don't know. Maybe." She set up three cardboard boxes, having already assessed my immediate pie needs. "He asked a lot of questions."

"About what? Your status? Your business?"

Her dirty blonde ponytail swished a negative. "About the murder. Everyone's talking about what you found on the trails."

"Already? It only happened an hour ago." I walked over to the window and scanned the parking lot. There were a couple of cars I didn't recognize, so I took a photo and blew it up. There was no sign of Justine, but she was on the move. I could feel it and Keats was still grumbling, too.

"The news hit the grapevine five minutes later. I've been fielding calls ever since." She sliced several pies and started moving pieces to the boxes. "There's gotta be a leak on the police force."

"Bunhead Betty, I bet. Maybe I can get Kellan to fire her. Did you hear about the dog crisis, too?"

"Dog crisis?" Mandy's pale blue eyes widened. She was always the first to hear the news. Very rarely did I get the jump on anyone.

After I explained, she wedged another slice of pie into an already full box. "You're going to need that. Thistledown doesn't have a bakery."

"You've been there before?"

She shook her head. "Dottie Bridges has a librarian colleague in Thistledown who comes to visit. Now that you and Dottie are besties, you could probably drop in on her friend to suss out the local news. Her name is Thelma Tilrow."

Dottie and I had started off as enemies and become something akin to friends. She'd been a big help in cracking more than one case and welcomed my visits, as long as I didn't bring livestock into the library. It was a reasonable, if not always achievable, request.

"I'll do that," I said. "Turns out I underestimated librarians. I bet everyone does."

She stacked the boxes and tied the pile with string. "Be careful, Ivy. This whole situation sounds strange. Don't turn your back on this Louisa."

"I won't. But if it helps, she did want three pieces of pie."

Mandy cocked her head. "That does help, actually. Goes to character."

I offered cash, as usual, and she declined, also as usual. In her mind, all the free pie in the world couldn't repay me for nearly getting me killed by her grandmother.

Lifting the stack of boxes, I smiled. "By that code I should have character to spare."

She smiled back at last. "You can never have too much."

"Of either pie or character," I said, letting Keats herd me back to the door. "Text me if you hear anything. And if Justine rears her annoying head."

"Already come and gone," Mandy said. "The chief is probably fending her off at the gravesite now."

Elbowing the door open, I stepped outside. "Doubtful. With Justine's navigational skills, she'll be lost in the trails for another hour. Plenty of time for us to beat it."

It was nice to hear Mandy's laughter as the door closed behind us. Nearly getting me murdered had turned her into one heck of a friend.

CHAPTER NINE

L ouisa was quiet on the hour-long drive, despite Jilly's
persistent efforts to draw her out. Our guest was determined to let her aunt tell the rest of the story about the missing
dog. And if Lou had a story of her own, she wasn't sharing it.

I could have jumped in to help with the interrogation but
my head was plenty full of my own stories. All of them ended
with the breeder trying to reclaim the dog who was rightfully
hers. While there was no microchip, she probably had plenty of
other proof of ownership.

Keats pulled his nose away from the passenger window and
shot me some warmth from his brown eye. Then he offered a
mumble of reassurance.

"Thanks, buddy," I said, reaching out to touch his side.

The exchange loosened Lou's tongue. "My aunt used to talk
to him, too. She said he talked back."

That drained the bit of confidence the dog had just given
me. I had expected my special connection to Keats to leave
Maud Gentry's in the dust.

He turned in Jilly's lap and rested a white paw on my hand
on the gearshift to show me nothing could beat our connection.

Nothing. We'd been put through the wringer and saved each other time and again.

Lou cleared her throat. "He saved her life, you know. My Aunt Maud's. Or so she told me."

My throat tightened up around the words I wanted to say so Jilly took up the cause. "What happened?"

"The first time, Aunt Maud was standing beside a river and someone ran up behind and shoved. Yeats—now, Keats—hauled her back by her coattails and then chased the attacker. The pup was just a few months old, but he got the job done. Nearly bit the guy's ear off."

My stomach did a slow turn. I thought Keats invented that move on my watch but it clearly came wired in. What's more, it killed my last shred of hope that this was a case of mistaken identity.

"That's how we knew for sure it was the right dog," Lou added helpfully. "The news coverage always focuses on how he bites ears. It's his signature move."

"Why did this guy attack your aunt?" Jilly asked.

"She'd turned him down for a puppy from previous litters. He had a grudge and a drinking problem. Makes for a deadly combo."

Jilly stroked Keats' side so rapidly I knew she was a little concerned. "Sounds like Keats showed early promise of what he became. A canine hero."

"I wish that was the only attack," Lou said. "Someone tried to run my aunt over a couple of times, too."

"Oh, wow. There's a target on Maud's back," Jilly said. "Why?"

Louisa sighed. "No reason, as far as I know. That's why I moved in with her. She really shouldn't live alone. And now even Frost is gone."

"Frost? That's Keats' sister?" I asked.

"Yeah. We call her Roberta Frost, after the poet."

"Quite the literary family," Jilly said. "Assuming you're named after the author, Louisa May Alcott."

"My mom was literary, but not Aunt Maud. I think she just likes strong, unique names."

At herding trials, many of the dogs had short powerful names, like Swift and Fate. Maybe that was from a time when all sheepdogs would be working in the field and one syllable carried. In my case, the name had been a personal preference. I hoped it didn't mean I'd have other things in common with this Maud, because if she had designs on my dog, I wanted to hate her.

"She's a quirky woman, my aunt," Lou said. "But if you try to keep an open mind, you'll like her."

Apparently, my mind was an open book to Louisa, who picked up on my thoughts nearly as well as Keats and Percy. Maybe it came of being descended from a sheepdog family. She'd acquired some of their traits, just as I had. Before Keats, I was never a woman of perpetual motion. My brain had one setting and it was steady. Now it was restless and fickle.

"Tell us about Frost," Jilly said. "Is she clever?"

"Yes. Very."

Interviewing her was like pulling teeth and we were far from novices.

"Knowing more about Frost would help us find her," I said. "And we need to see a photo."

After pondering for a moment, she stuck her phone through the seats. A quick glance showed me a border collie with very different coloring to Keats. The dog's fur was brown with bronze and white accents.

"Oh my, she's so pretty," Jilly said, taking the phone and enlarging the photo. "Her eyes look green."

"They are. Most of the pups in each litter were typical, but these two stood out in both looks and smarts. Aunt Maud said they practically trained themselves."

"And their mother?" Jilly asked. "She must have been special, too."

"We don't talk about her anymore," Lou said. "My aunt's never been the same since she lost that dog."

Keats gave a rumble that suggested we back off the interrogation. Maybe he didn't want to dwell on the loss of his mother either.

Jilly and I took the hint and we traveled the last leg of the journey in silence.

"Here we are," Jilly said, probably relieved to have something safe to talk about. "Isn't it quaint?"

Thistledown may not have been much of a town but what there was of it was pleasant. It was everything Clover Grove aspired to be but couldn't quite achieve. My hometown had started as little more than a farming outpost and its roots showed. The oldest buildings were utilitarian. Sensible. Devoid of charm. Since Dorset Hills became popular with its Dog Town branding, we'd chased the same golden ring hard and fast. There was a trying-too-hard vibe on our Main Street, at least to someone who'd known the place before the copycat antique-style signs went up over every store.

The small Thistledown core consisted of a scattering of stores that had clearly been repurposed. The hardware store had once been a smithy, judging by the hitching posts outside, and the diner a general store. The tavern had probably always been a saloon of one type or another.

We were already through the town and out the other side before I thought to look for the library. If I had time, I wanted to pop in and say hello to Dottie's friend.

"Turn left here," Lou said. "Last house on the right."

The yellow brick bungalow was neat and unassuming.

There were several planters containing limp and saggy chrysan-themums. Frost had taken them down, and not the canine kind.

A woman came out on the porch who didn't look quirky at all by my standards, which were admittedly lax. She was wearing pressed jeans with a straight white crease down the front, a shirt with a subdued floral pattern, and black loafers. Her gray hair was tied in a short ponytail and her eyes were as blue as her niece's. She could have been anyone from the regular rank and file of Clover Grove's female population of my mother's vintage. In my experience, quirky showed itself in long braids, ponchos, camouflage or, in Mom's case, scarlet satin and boas.

Louisa hopped out of the truck and ran up the stairs to hug her aunt, who stepped back to avoid the affection. The move was familiar to me. The Galloways were not a warm family, at least on the surface.

Gertie's van pulled onto the gravel shoulder, leaving my truck room to roll out of the driveway fast if I needed to escape. That was the kind of affection I valued. As Jilly and I walked to the stairs, I signaled my senior friends to give us a moment. This could be a sensitive conversation and diplomacy wasn't in Edna's wheelhouse.

After making hasty introductions, Lou scanned her aunt's face. "I take it Frost hasn't come home."

"Not yet." Maud's lips pressed together in a thin line and she blinked rapidly. I suspected hating her was already out of the question. She was so heartbroken over her missing dog she could barely conceal it.

"Where is he?" she said, looking past me to the truck. "Yeats."

"Keats," I said. "I prefer the romantic poets. Yeats' work was dark. Bleak."

Maud's lips turned down. "I don't go in for such foolishness. It's just a solid name."

"Like Roberta Frost," I said, fighting the urge to smirk and failing.

She turned a glare on her niece. "I told you not to talk too much."

"She tried not to," Jilly said. "But getting stuck in a tree and questioned by cops would loosen anyone's lips."

"A tree? Cops? What on earth happened, Lou?" Maud's voice reminded me of a crow. Harsh. Grating. "You had a very simple task. To find this woman and bring my dog home."

"*My* dog," I said. My tone was firm. Even defiant. If I didn't like what Maud said next, Keats wasn't leaving the truck. And we were leaving town.

The older woman seemed to have the same skill as her niece at reading my thoughts because her expression softened. "I meant Frost. For the record, I call all the dogs I've bred 'my' dogs. But Keats is in your care." Just as my shoulders started to relax, she added, "Unless he'd prefer to stay with us."

"He wouldn't," Jilly said, crisply. "He has a wonderful home at Runaway Farm and is beloved by many."

"A wonderful home that constantly puts him in peril." Maud tried to intimidate Jilly with a stare but it would take more than that to cow my friend. "He's not safe."

"Just like he wasn't safe before," I said. "Almost got shoved into a river, apparently. And then got stolen from right under your nose. And now Frost is gone, too. At least I still have my dog, Miss Gentry."

Her Adam's apple bobbed up and down. It was surprisingly prominent for a woman. "Touché."

Louisa turned on me. "You don't need to be so mean. Can you imagine how it feels to lose a dog like Frost?"

Maud's hand dropped onto her shoulder. "Of course, she can, Lou. That's why she's being so—"

"Mean," Lou supplied.

"Assertive," her aunt corrected. "I not only understand but respect her stance. She's going to fight for that dog."

"You bet I am. And he's not getting out of that truck until you promise you won't try to kidnap him or even woo him with your breederly charms. This dog keeps me sane. And alive. I will fight to the death for him. Just so you know."

"Ivy's a good warrior," Edna said, coming up behind me. "Not elite level, but she could take you and Louisa here down just like that." She snapped her camo-gloved fingers soundlessly. "Plus she'd never fight alone."

Maud scanned Edna and Gertie and her faint silvery eyebrows rose. "Interesting. I respect that my dog—the dog—has good backing."

I crossed my arms and conveyed a silent message.

The breeder only held her ground for a second. "*Your* dog, I mean."

"You do have a claim on him, Auntie," Lou said. "You can prove in half a dozen ways he was yours. Genetic testing, for starters."

"The only way that counts is his choice," Maud said. "And his eyes haven't left Ivy since she got out of the truck. Reclaiming him would equal abuse, in my mind, regardless of the law. I brought him into the world to be happy, and apparently he is."

Finally, my muscles started to unclench and I nodded to Gertie. "You can let them all out."

Keats leapt from the driver's door, took a couple of bounds and catapulted into my arms. He was not a dog for blatant PDAs and preferred to have four on the floor, as Cori Hogan, expert dog trainer, liked to say. This move was very clearly a statement to his first owner that I was his last.

"It's all right, Yeats, I get it," Maud said. "No need to be so dramatic."

He mumbled something in her general direction from my arms.

"Fine, then. *Keats*. I never liked the poet's verse much. But I do like you."

I felt the tip of my dog's tail flop against my leg. "Would you like to go and say hello to Maud? I won't cry."

"Nor will I," Maud said. "Although I'll be the first to admit my nerves are stretched pretty thin over Frost."

I set Keats down and he went up the stairs to stand at his breeder's feet. His tail swished in submission but his ears and eyes were alert. He had loved her once, it seemed, but he loved me more. Unless I was much mistaken, he felt a little guilty about that. It wasn't his fault he was taken from her, but he had indeed made a choice to embrace a new life with me.

My eyes met Maud's over the dog and we exchanged small smiles. Both of us had lied because both of us cried.

Percy chased our awkwardness away by pursuing Fanny up the stairs with another hiss. The gray cat climbed onto her owner's shoulder and blinked at us. There was a smugness on her pretty feline face that made me wonder if Percy was getting played.

"I'll get your dog back, Miss Gentry, I promise," I said. "Frost, I mean. It's the least I can do to thank you for the most amazing gift of my life."

Keats recovered himself enough to give a mumble-brag.

"You weren't always so full of yourself, young man," she said. Then she straightened and nodded. "I know you two—and the rest of you—will bring Frost home. I'm counting on it."

CHAPTER TEN

It was closing in on noon so we let Maud brief us quickly, then devised a plan and deployed without fanfare. Edna and Gertie decided to search on foot with Louisa, who knew the area well. Maud stayed home to await Frost, and field calls from the few volunteers who'd come forward after seeing the "lost dog" signs Louisa had posted.

Jilly and I wanted to interview the dog-sitter and see where that led.

"Can I come with you guys?" Lou said, as Edna and Gertie started marching away. "Those two scare me."

"Good," Edna called back. "You're not as devoid of sense as you seemed."

"Edna, lighten up," Jilly said. "Louisa isn't used to your jokes."

"I'm just stating the obvious. This girl is meant for city life. A soldier she'll never be."

"We were city girls, too," Jilly said. "It only took a year to transform."

"Less," I said. "The city leaked out of me the first time someone tried to kill me in my own barn."

Louisa flinched. "Do you have to talk about that?"

"Isn't that why you came for us? To access our specialized skill set?" I zipped my jacket and sighed. "Talking about it is healthier than pretending it didn't happen."

"Move it or lose us," Edna yelled. "We don't indulge whiners on our team."

Finally, Keats drove Lou in the direction of my warrior friends and she hopped off, quite literally.

Blowing out a sigh of relief, I whispered, "Thank goodness. She drains my emotional battery."

We headed down the road toward the house Maud had pointed out. Percy trotted ahead with his tail up, glad to be free of both the crate and Fanny.

"No wonder," Jilly said, "when she reminds you regularly that Keats had a life before you."

"I suppose returning him would be the honorable thing to do. It's not Maud's fault someone stole him from that dog show." The quaver was back in my voice and soft ears arrived under my fingertips. "But I can't."

"You can't and she doesn't expect that." Jilly touched my arm. "She said so herself. Don't worry about it."

"What if she changes her mind? If we can't find Frost, for example. You saw how attached she is to that dog and she might want to fill the hole with mine."

Keats gave a low mumble that dared her to try. Still, I detected that note of sadness again. No doubt he had some nostalgia about their time together. Maud wasn't warm with humans but I knew well that a crusty surface could hide a deep love of animals. I used to be crusty myself, but my animals—this dog in particular—had cracked open the heart I tried hard to protect in the corporate world.

"It won't happen. We won't let it." Jilly smiled. "Gertie could let Minnie handle the job."

That thought perked me up. "And Edna could give her pepper spray a workout on Louisa. She's annoying."

"I guess she's afraid," Jilly said. "Not only for the dog but her aunt's safety. And she seems rather alone in the world. You know as well as I do that people aren't themselves when they're terrified."

I nodded. "I'm terrified half the time. I don't even know myself anymore. It's a miracle I haven't driven everyone away."

"On the contrary. You pull people toward you like a magnet."

"Not all of them good, obviously. My gravitational field seems to attract some debris. By the time I'm Edna's age, I'll have rings like Saturn."

We were both laughing as we went up the front walk, which was a much better state of mind to begin an investigation.

Darnese Bibb came out onto the porch before we reached the stairs. She was still in her flannel pajamas and a paisley housecoat that had seen better years. Her short, salt and pepper hair stuck up all over and did little to soften her sharp features and small dark eyes.

"I'm so glad to see you," she said. "And I apologize for being such a mess. I haven't had a moment's peace since I woke up and found the dog missing. Maud believes you can set this to rights and I sincerely hope that's true. Otherwise, she'll never speak to me again. She trusted me and now look what I've done. I've lost her treasured dog."

She twisted something in her hands over and over. It was a brown leather leash that probably belonged to Frost.

"It's okay, Mrs. Bibb," Jilly said, offering a kind smile. "I'm sure we'll get this figured out. Can you tell us what happened?"

I expected her to invite us in but she didn't. Instead, she kept twisting the leash and scanning the street with red-rimmed brown eyes, likely hoping the border collie would lope into view.

"Girls, I'm totally baffled. Everything was fine when I went to bed. I took Frost out for her last call at 10 and left her in the kitchen curled up on her bed. When I came out this morning before six, she was gone. All the doors and windows were still locked, including the basement, and nothing was taken but the dog."

"Who else has a key?" I asked, sending Keats toward her with a twitch of my fingers. "They had to get in somehow."

"Only my daughter, Sunny," she said. "After my son moved out a few years ago, I changed the locks. He was hanging with a bad crowd, but last I heard, he straightened himself out and was in Boston with a good job."

"And what did Sunny have to say about what happened to Frost?" I asked.

"She rushed over here at the crack of dawn and searched for hours before her shift. We've known Maud for more than a year and looked after the dog a couple of times. Frost loves Sunny and would have come if she was in earshot."

Keats walked up the stairs slowly, telling an interesting tale with his tail. It started out low, rose and bristled, and then settled about midway. I read it to mean that Darnese wasn't being entirely up front with us.

"We'd like to take a look around," I said. "Sometimes my dog sees or smells things others can't."

My cat was no slouch, either. He slipped past Darnese without her even noticing as she opened the door.

"I've been over and over the house and so has Sunny," she said, leading us through the small living room and into the kitchen. The place was neat and clean but dated and a little shabby. "I highly doubt you'll find anything."

Keats tried to get a good whiff of the leash but her hands kept moving restlessly.

"Would you mind letting my dog sniff the lead?" I asked. "He never met Frost. According to Maud, she was a full sister from a subsequent litter."

"Of course," she said, offering it to him, palm up. "Nothing would make me happier than reuniting them."

I believed her. No matter what she wasn't disclosing, she sincerely wished the best for the missing dog.

Keats inspected the leash closely and the white tip of his tail flicked. It seemed like a confirmation about Frost's identity. At the very least, it was a dog he wished to know better. That wasn't always the case. He had little patience for most dogs, with the notable exceptions of Byron, our livestock guardian, and Cori's sheepdog, Clem.

I reached out to take the leash and slipped it into the pocket of my overalls. If we found Frost—*when* we found her—it would likely be comforting to have something on hand that smelled of Maud and home.

Darnese turned, then clutched her throat and gave a little scream when she saw Percy on the kitchen counter. He was rubbing his orange fluff against a tall red tin. "What's in there?" I asked. "My cat is awfully interested."

"Frost's kibble," she said, reaching for the tin. Her eyes bulged as she lifted it. "Oh, goodness. It's empty."

"So, we have a clue," I said. "Someone was in here and took the food as well as the dog. At least they don't intend to starve her."

"Impossible," Darnese said. "There was no sign at all of forced entry."

"And you don't leave a key out? Most people do."

"Not in Thistledown, they don't. We've had spells of break-ins going back as far as I can remember. They die off and then start again." She rubbed her face with both hands. "At one time, people blamed my son, Kale, but it continued long after he was gone. Hill country used to be so safe, but times have changed."

"In Clover Grove, too," I said, heading for the back door. Keats was avidly sniffing the mat and mumbled to let me know it was worth a look outside. "And thieves lifted something valuable here today."

She started to offer another protest, then stopped. Frost might have walked out of here on her own but the kibble didn't.

"I've been out there a dozen times, looking for signs," she said. "The gate was closed and latched, just like always."

Keats and Percy did a full circuit of the yard, with the cat pacing along the top, tail lashing. He was unhappy about something and I had no doubt he'd share it with us soon.

Sure enough, when Percy reached the gate, he gave a swish of his orange paw. His claws weren't flexed, so I didn't take it as an absolute pronouncement of doom. However, it wasn't a joyful gesture, either.

Meanwhile, Keats stood on his hind legs, sniffing. The sound that came out of him next wasn't a mumble but a whine.

Jilly and I rushed over to see what had troubled the boys, and it didn't take long to locate the source. Caught in the gate's latch was a tuft of brown fur with a few strands of white. Dried blood stained the metal.

CHAPTER ELEVEN

Jilly gasped and clasped her hands together. "Poor Frost has been injured. Maud will be heartbroken."

"Someone must have carried the dog out this way," I said, using a bandana from my pocket to release the latch. "She must have been struggling. Panicking." My throat tightened as I imagined the sheepdog resisting. "She could have just bitten the thief. Why didn't she?"

"She's a very gentle dog," Darnese said. "I've never had a moment's trouble with her until..." Her voice drifted off and then she added, "I'm sure she'll be fine. If they intended to harm her, they wouldn't have taken her kibble. Like you said."

Keats dropped to all fours and turned to stare at Darnese with his blue eye. It must have made her uncomfortable because she angled slightly away.

I dug into my HR tool chest and forced my lips into a smile. "Mrs. Bibb, it sounds like you had some trouble with Frost yesterday. We understand things happen with animals. You can tell us about it."

She angled even further away but Keats circled and eased

her around with a nudge that would become holes in her house-coat if she didn't comply.

"It was nothing I couldn't handle," she said. "I've owned dogs all my life and she wasn't the first to try to escape."

"Ah. So this blood on the latch... it came from her trying to jump over the fence?"

Her ruffled hair fluttered in an almost imperceptible nod. "Never known her to try that before. But I was standing right here and caught her in time. She's very springy."

She tried to pat her hair into place, revealing a trio of scratches on her forearm.

"Looks like Frost put up quite a fight when you caught her," I said, gesturing to the scratches.

Her arm dropped and the sleeve fell over the wounds. "It's nothing."

"It's something," I said. "I've never been scratched like that before by Frost's brother."

Her eyes became pleading. "Please don't upset Maud over this. Yes, the dog tried to make a run for it, but I caught her. End of story."

"Except it's not," Jilly said gently. "Later, she was gone. Is there a chance she escaped, rather than being stolen?"

"Absolutely not," Darnese said. "I checked every door and window at bedtime, because she's good with knobs and latches."

"So she has tried to escape before," I said.

"Just once. Maybe twice. Never like this."

"Like what?" I prompted.

She covered her eyes and sighed. "Like someone was after her. When I was the only one here. The other times, she was half-hearted. I figured she just wanted to run home and look for Maud. This time really was different. If I hadn't caught her in time she'd have crested that fence like an Olympian high jumper."

"What happened after that?" Jilly asked.

Pulling a tattered white handkerchief out of her pocket, Darnese patted her eyes. "I took Frost inside, of course. Never let her out again without a leash. We couldn't take a walk because I didn't trust her to behave."

"What about Frost's wound?" I pointed to her patterned housecoat. "There's blood on your robe. Quite a bit of it, now that I'm looking. You must have noticed."

"It was just a little cut on her shoulder. Nothing serious, so I dressed it myself." Dabbing at her eyes again, she added, "She was completely fine."

I sighed. "Maud is going to be devastated to know her beloved dog is on the run with an open wound. And that you decided not to mention it."

"Maybe the local police will take more interest now," Jilly said. "If not, at least ours will."

"Your what?" Darnese said.

"Our police," I said. "Chief Harper from Clover Grove offered to send an officer down. Jilly's husband, perhaps."

"Or your fiancé," Jilly said. "The chief himself."

"Surely that's overkill," Darnese said. "When our own police said it wasn't worth investigating."

Keats was back under my fingertips and he grumbled quite loudly.

"Here's the thing, Darnese," I said. "The chief considers Keats family, and by extension, Frost is family, too. We couldn't live with ourselves if we stood by wringing our hands while she ran around injured. Judging by the fur and blood, she needs to get to a vet quickly."

Darnese let out a sigh that was a mixture of indignation and resignation. "Well, you can stop your fussing. She saw a vet and really is fine."

I looked at Jilly and then pulled my phone out of my pocket.

"It seems like there's a lot you didn't tell Maud. Is there more, or would you be more comfortable speaking directly to my fiancé? He's awfully busy at the moment but I'm sure he'll spare a moment for Keats' family."

"No, I don't want to speak to your fiancé," she said. "As much as you like throwing that word around."

That brought the first pant-laugh out of Keats since our arrival in Thistledown. I couldn't help smiling, too. I did like that word. In fact, it was my new favorite word. I hadn't had much of a chance to use it, let alone throw it around. But if it helped find an animal in need, you could bet I would exploit the word "fiancé" to the fullest. Kellan wouldn't mind a bit. On the contrary, he'd be quite gratified.

"He's very nice," I said. "No need to be intimidated by the title. Although he does get impatient when people lie about hurting animals."

She snapped her handkerchief with a flourish. "I did not hurt that dog. All I did was catch her as she tried to escape. Then I took her down to the animal clinic to get the gash checked. At my own expense, too."

"You brought Frost straight home after that?"

"On her leash. She never left my sight. And then we sat around all day watching soap operas." Patting her forehead with the hankie, she added, "Maybe your fiancé could check my TV log, if he's so inclined."

"Maybe," I said. "What they can do with modern technology astounds me."

"I've told you everything I know," she said, and the hankie dropped from her fingers to the grass.

I doubted that highly. The story had more twists than any soap opera, but with her agitation increasing, I knew we needed to ease off.

Keats obviously agreed because he circled to press Jilly and me toward the gate.

Percy took a leap off the fence and landed lightly on the grass in front of Darnese. She let out a startled squawk but she wasn't the cat's target. Instead, he swept a paw over the fallen hankie.

Once, twice, three times.

The frayed cloth was getting a proper litter box burial, claws included.

"What is he doing?" Darnese asked.

I opened the gate and signaled Keats to collect Percy. "Just saying it needs a wash, I think. Cats are so finicky."

We left her muttering indignantly and followed the animals down the lane.

CHAPTER TWELVE

I t was a short walk into town so we didn't bother going back to Maud's house for the truck. I preferred to avoid her as much as I could. When we'd successfully recovered her dog, I'd feel a lot more confident she wouldn't make an end run on mine. The case was a little more complicated than I'd hoped but at least it didn't involve a murder. Kellan could deal with the gangster graveyard back home. It would probably keep him busy right through Thanksgiving, unfortunately.

Up the street a stretch, a white-haired man was raking the last of the fall leaves off his front lawn. He gave us a wave, but when his eyes landed on Keats and Percy, he came to the gravel strip at the edge of the road.

"What a fine-looking dog," he said. "Is it one of Maud Gentry's?"

"Apparently, yes," I said. "I didn't know that till this morning when her niece came to look me up. We're trying to locate Frost."

His brow furrowed and he pushed his glasses back up his nose. Silver duct tape bound the frames together at the bridge.

There was a dark bruise on one cheek that suggested a recent collision between his face and a foreign object.

"This is one of the stolen ones, then," he said. "Before Frost."

"So it would seem, sir," I said.

"Call me Elmer. Elmer Mogus."

His hand had a long scratch, so I clasped it gently while making the introductions. Percy and Keats stared at him, wide-eyed. He was definitely cause for curiosity.

"Other than mine, how many of Maud's dogs were stolen, Elmer?" I asked. I was starting to wonder if we were getting the straight goods from anyone.

"Maud's? One more that I know of," Elmer said. "I'm not sure they were all stolen, actually, as Frost was behind her own disappearance."

"How so?"

He gestured to his face. "That's how I got banged up. I managed to corner Frost in my yard yesterday. Picked her up but she fought like a badger."

"What time of day was this, Mr. Mogus?" I asked.

"Around noon, I guess. Her paw was in a surgical dressing but she nailed me good with the other three."

"Her paw? I thought Frost had a cut on her shoulder."

"All I know is she was wearing a little blue boot on her right front paw," he said.

"And she got away?"

"Did my best but she tipped me over and bolted." He pointed behind his house. "Last seen heading into the bush."

"Oh, the poor thing," Jilly said. "It sounds like she was beside herself with either pain or terror."

"Maybe disoriented," I said. "And looking for Maud."

Elmer shook his head. "Sure seemed like she knew what she was doing. She wasn't going to let anyone stand in her way."

"How strange," I said. "Any idea why people would go after Maud's dogs? I mean, I know my dog is amazing, but there's an odd pattern here."

Starting to rake again, he let his glasses slip down. "Some say Maud has enemies. That she came here to hide."

"Do those people ever say why? She seems like an upstanding citizen to me."

"And Louisa, too," Jilly added, earning a noncommittal mumble from Keats. The jury was still out on Lou, possibly because she'd successfully tailed us earlier when he was otherwise engaged in tailing Edna and Gertie.

"Guess it depends on what you consider upstanding," he said. "Maud's called the township on me before."

"Why would she do that?" Jilly asked. "You seem like an upstanding citizen, too."

He nodded and his glasses landed at the tip of his nose. "I like to think so. If my greatest crime is putting bread out for the birds, I can live with that."

"She called in a complaint over feeding the birds?" I asked.

The glasses dropped off with his next nod. He caught them, losing his grip on the rake in the process. "Sent a wildlife control officer over to inspect my property." Putting his glasses back on, he stared at me. "We don't even have wildlife control here. They had to bring the guy in from another region. Just to menace an old man and his breadcrusts."

"I'm so sorry to hear that," Jilly said. "We love birds, too. All animals, actually."

Percy leapt and her arms automatically reached out to catch him.

Finally, Elmer smiled. "I can see that."

I wanted to give Maud the benefit of the doubt. It was hard to believe the woman who produced Keats was so reactive to what seemed like a simple thing.

"Any idea why Maud got so upset over feeding the birds?" I asked.

"Just a hothead. Said attracting wildlife would put her dog at risk." Anchoring the glasses, he bent to pick up the fallen rake. "As if a raccoon or two could cause that much trouble."

"Rabies is always a risk, I suppose," I said. "Their droppings carry other diseases."

"Raccoons deserve to eat, too," he said, straightening. "And foxes. They're all worthy in my books. If she wants to live in a castle, she can build a moat. Or move to the city."

"I understand your concern," Jilly said, always the diplomat. "After losing previous dogs, Maud must have been extra worried about Frost."

"Look how well that worked out. The second she went away, the dog bolted." He gestured to Keats. "I'd say Frost is looking for a new owner, just like this one did."

Keats gave a mumble of dissent. He hadn't left Maud by choice. He was torn away from his first home and had a miserable existence till I came along. I certainly hoped Frost wasn't facing a similar fate.

"That's not quite how it happened," I said. "Someone stole my pup from a dog show and I rescued him from a criminal. A murderer, in fact."

His eyebrows rose. It felt like a long time since I'd surprised anyone with my story. If news circulated that slowly in Thistledown, it was no wonder Maud had moved here. I couldn't even imagine the freedom of living outside the glare of the Clover Grove rumor mill.

"Maybe Maud was ready to breed Frost," I said. "Start fresh. All the more reason to worry about health and safety."

"I want one of those puppies," Jilly said.

Keats made a huffing noise and Elmer laughed. "Someone doesn't like that idea very much from the sounds of it."

Jilly looked at Keats and smiled. "We may not be sharing a roof forever, Keats. How am I to get on without you?"

The dog gave a mumble that suggested he was dog enough to cover two households. It was true, but eventually, when Jilly's family expanded, she probably would need a dog of her own. It was odd that it had never occurred to me before. She hadn't particularly liked pets when we moved to Clover Grove, but now I couldn't imagine her without at least a cat. And honestly, with the threats we faced, she needed a dog, too.

The indignant mumble came again.

"No one could compare with you, buddy," she said. "But some of us need to settle for less."

"There will be a lot of competition for those pups if they ever arrive," Elmer said. "Frost is the smartest dog I've ever met. Normally calm, too, for a sheepdog. But there was a bee in her bonnet yesterday and I hope she shakes it loose."

"According to Darnese Bibb, she was locked up safely last night." I watched him closely for a reaction. "I hope that's true."

He turned his back and started raking. "Probably. And other things are probably also true. That's how these things go."

He was right. I used to think there was one truth but I hadn't been that naïve in a long time.

Keats started to round Jilly and me up and I pulled a business card out of my front pocket. "Would you please call me if you see any signs of Frost?"

Taking the card, he nodded. "I'll leave the wrangling to you or those ladies you sent into the bush. Strange pair."

I laughed. "You don't know the half of it."

Elmer took in my overalls with a little shake of his head. Even Jilly's jeans and nice jacket evidently failed to pass muster.

"Women were women in my day." He pursed his lips and turned back to his raking.

We started to move off, with Keats steering from behind. "A lot's changed in hill country, sir," I called over my shoulder.

"And even more's stayed the same," he called back. "Not all of it good."

CHAPTER THIRTEEN

The vet technician came to collect us from the waiting room right away. We had Percy to thank for that, because he'd taken the liberty of pushing an interior door open and going to fetch her. He was still wearing his yellow bomber, which made him hard to miss, and turned on his motor, too. Without Fanny around, he was all charm again.

"What a beautiful cat," she said, as he swished around the legs of her blue uniform. "The dog is gorgeous, too."

Keats mumbled an acknowledgement. He'd received plenty of compliments today but I doubted he'd rest on his laurels. We were all very much aware that each passing hour would make it harder to find Frost, especially if the prediction of overnight snow came to fruition.

Her nametag said Zoe Hampton and despite her surgical scrubs, she had a trendy city vibe. "Thanks, Zoe. They both appreciate flattery, especially in a vet's office. Everyone gets a little nervous, am I right?"

"Most, I'm afraid," she said. "Do you have an appointment?"

"Actually, it's just a walk-in. Hoping you might have a few minutes."

She beckoned. "You're in luck. Someone booked me to express anal glands and cancelled last minute. For their cocker spaniel, that is."

Keats' prance seemed a little stiffer than usual, although he'd never had anal gland trouble. In fact, he rarely needed to see a vet, despite our adventures.

His tail came up again to suggest he liked Zoe Hampton's vibe. That was a relief. On a day when people seemed extra slippery, it was nice to think we might catch a break here.

We all went into a bright room at the back of the clinic. There was an examination table, a counter with a sink, and a couple of chairs. Zoe gestured for Jilly and me to take the chairs, and leaned against the counter. Percy leapt lightly onto the exam table and paraded back and forth until she fell for his ploy and started scratching his chin. His best purr roared out again and it seemed to put the technician at ease.

That faded quickly, however, after I made the introductions. Her heavily lined dark eyes darted from one of us to the other and then around the room. She tossed shiny black hair over her shoulders and then brought it forward again.

"Who's in trouble, today?" she asked, using her free hand to point from the cat to the dog. "I assume it's a little worse than impacted anal glands."

"That sets the bar high," I said, offering a mid-range HR smile. There was no need to squander my best resources when they might be needed later. I had a feeling it was going to be a long day. "Happily, both my pets are healthy. It's Keats' sister we're worried about."

"Sister?" Her finely penciled eyebrows rose and stayed in flight.

I nodded. "Frost Gentry. We heard from Darnese Bibb that Frost was here about a gash she got while trying to jump over a fence."

Zoe straightened and crossed her arms. "I can't discuss our patients. Or their owners, for that matter. The veterinarian has a privacy policy."

"Understandable," I said. "I'm here on behalf of Frost's owner, Maud. Let's just get her on the phone to give the required consent."

Her eyes darted around some more and Percy worked his head butt on her midriff to calm her down. It must have worked because she looked back at me. "That won't be necessary. Frost didn't need to see the veterinarian. Just me. I was going to call Maud about it later. After..."

Her voice drifted off and Jilly picked up for her. "After Frost came home. As you can imagine, Maud's very upset right now. Knowing Frost is injured will only make things worse."

"The cut was superficial," Zoe said. "I cleaned it up and she was good to go."

"What about her paw?" I asked. "A neighbor said she was wearing a blue dressing."

Now Zoe's eyes filled with tears. "That part is my fault. And I'm so afraid to tell Maud."

"It's okay. We'll cushion the blow for her," I said. "Frost was getting around fine after she saw you. Elmer Mogus said she gave him a good thumping."

"Accidents happen," Jilly added. "Did Frost jump off the table?"

Zoe shook her head. "It wasn't that. She tried to claw her way out the back door and broke a nail."

"Yikes," I said. "I know that bleeds a lot."

"So much. It was all over my smock. Something out of a horror movie."

"Because you tried to restrain her?" Jilly asked. "She resisted?"

"Yeah." Tears flowed down Zoe's cheeks, along with

eyeliner and mascara. "I love Frost. She's normally so gentle and calm."

"Maybe she was trying to escape Darnese," I said. "The upset started in her yard."

"Maybe. But honestly, it didn't seem like the Frost I know. She was determined to escape. It was all I could do to get her bandaged before she... Well, you know what happened."

"She obviously broke out of here," I said. "Since Elmer saw her around noon."

Zoe ran her hands through her hair, one after another. "I knew Frost was good with doorhandles and I should have slid the bolt. While Darnese and I were talking about how to manage the bandage, Frost let herself out and took off."

"On her injured foot," I said. "That takes commitment."

"Shot away like lightning. I've never seen a faster dog."

Keats mumbled a cocky challenge to that. The sibling rivalry had apparently begun even before their first meeting.

"Can you think of any reason she'd be so motivated to bolt?" I asked.

Zoe walked over to the back door and opened it, probably hoping the dog had returned to the scene of the jailbreak. "I wondered if she might be in heat and determined to get herself hitched. They can act a little crazy at that point. But in that case, Maud wouldn't have left her with a novice like Darnese."

"Interesting theory and worth exploring," I said. "Did Darnese go after Frost?"

"We both did." She brightened a little. "I searched over my lunch break, but then Sunny texted me and said they'd found her. That's Darnese's daughter."

Jilly and I glanced at each other. "Did you believe her?"

Zoe pulled a tissue out of her pocket and mopped up black streaks on her cheeks. "Sure. Sunny and I have known each other since kindergarten. We were good friends. Plus, she sent me a photo."

Percy was on the counter behind Zoe now and he sent her phone spinning before catching my eye.

"Could we see the photo?" I asked. "It might help to see the time stamp and the background. We're putting the pieces together."

She fiddled with her phone and then offered it to me. Sure enough, there was a selfie of a blonde woman kneeling beside Frost on a sidewalk outside the tavern. The dog's ears were flat and she didn't look at all happy about being locked down again. Still, I was taken by her beauty, and a grumble near my shins protested my disloyalty.

After snapping a photo of the screen, I handed Zoe's phone back, and zipped my jacket again.

Jilly touched my arm to slow me down. "Zoe, you said you used to be good friends with Sunny. Did you grow apart? Happens all the time. Ivy's the only friend I've managed to hold onto."

Her eyes dropped to Jilly's ring finger and then hopped to mine, widening when she saw the rubber washer. "Guys never pulled you apart?"

"No, but that happened to me in high school a few times," Jilly said. "Before we knew better than to put any guy first. At that stage, boyfriends come and go whereas friends can last forever."

"Exactly! That's always been my rule," Zoe said. "But Sunny started seeing some guy maybe a month ago and stopped returning my calls. When I went to talk to her at Fresh Pickens, where she works, she was pretty chilly. I could barely get a cheese sample."

"No explanation at all?" Jilly asked.

Zoe's eyes teared up again. "She said everything was fine. That she was just busy."

Percy jumped down to join Keats at the back door, so I assumed we'd learned all we could here.

"I bet Sunny comes back around," Jilly said. "You're a loyal friend and she'll realize it."

"I hope so. If she does, the door's still open."

Keats took that as his cue to rise on his back paws and unlatch the door. I'd never seen him do that before, although it didn't particularly surprise me. All it took was a little competition to make it happen. Oddly, the fact that he cared about matching his sister's skills reassured me Frost was still alive and well. He would want to rub her nose in his talents when she surfaced.

"Make sure you look for her down by the pond," Zoe called after us as we went out into the parking lot.

"Sunny?" I called back.

"Frost. That's where Maud takes her in the evening to do their drills. It's their happy place."

Doing drills probably wasn't fun for most dogs, but I could see that it would be for a border collie without a farm to run.

Keats mumbled something insolent that sounded like, "Loser."

"Zip it, buddy," Jilly said, when we were out of Zoe's earshot. "Frost is your sister. A blood relative. As an only child I'd suggest that's worth something."

I grinned at her. "As the youngest of six I'd say blood's overrated."

Keats frolicked around us, his angst over the coat forgotten.

For the moment, anyway.

CHAPTER FOURTEEN

There wasn't much more to Thistledown's main drag than we'd seen that morning but some of the side streets were lined with pretty stores, and towering trees. The budget for policing seemed to have been reallocated to landscaping and design. Their Thanksgiving decorations were so ornate they rivaled those of Dorset Hills, the holiday capital of hill country.

It wouldn't have been hard to find Fresh Pickens even if Keats hadn't led us directly to the store. The smells of coffee and cheese were bait for tourists.

At least, for tourists who hadn't eaten a lot of pie during the drive from Clover Grove. Jilly had held the box and I used my fingers. Desperate times called for desperate measures.

Sunny Bibb was behind the cheese counter when we arrived. She was less attractive in person than in the photo she'd sent Zoe, where her small dark eyes and pointy features had been softened with artfully arranged tresses. The hairnet she wore today would flatter no one. A sullen expression didn't help. No doubt Darnese had sent out an alert that we were on the prowl.

"No pets in the store, ma'am," she said, as we walked up to her station.

I glanced at Jilly. "You must be the ma'am, because you're already married."

"Au contraire. The title applies to the owner of the pets," Jilly said. "But I'm willing to take the hit. What are friends for?"

"It's not the worst hit you've taken for me."

"Not by far, my friend. I'd need all day to sort through that list and come up with a winner."

"Ma'ams," Sunny said. "Plural. I think you're missing the point about the pets."

"Sorry," I said. "We got caught up in your delivery. Jilly and I have been friends for so long, you see."

"Like you and Zoe Hampton," Jilly said. "Ivy and I always have each other's back, even when it comes to titles like ma'am."

Color flooded into the salesclerk's cheeks. "Zoe and I are good friends. But people grow apart sometimes. Our careers are taking us in different directions."

I didn't figure selling cheese was the type of career to break up a friendship, but it wasn't my place to judge. There may well have been more to Sunny than Keats let on with his lackluster posture.

He mumbled that he'd offered full disclosure. And further-more, that Sunny didn't smell much better than the cheese.

I fought a decidedly non-HR approved grin and Jilly took over for me. "I'm sure you and Zoe will go the distance," she said. "In a town this small, friends are probably in short supply."

Sunny propped her elbows on the counter. "What did she say about me?"

"Just that you found Frost yesterday and texted the good news," I said. "She was happy and relieved."

"All of us were. My mom especially."

I moved a little closer to study her reactions. "How did you manage to find the dog? She covered a lot of ground."

"I had to ask my boss if I could leave early, then I combed the streets. Frost moves fast and I didn't hold out much hope, but after a couple of hours, I found her sitting outside the library."

"How was her paw?" Jilly asked.

"The bandage was on, thank goodness." I could see Sunny meant it. Her sullen attitude didn't extend to the dog. "Dirty, but still stuck in place. Zoe did a good job on it."

All of us seemed to sigh at once and it lifted the dark cloud enough that I could press on. "So then what happened? You just leashed her and walked home?"

"I wish." She unbuttoned the store uniform at the neck and showed us a series of bruises around her clavicle. "I didn't have her leash, so I carried her. She beat the living blazes out of me. Used the bandage like a boxing glove."

"But she knows you, doesn't she?" Jilly said.

"Definitely. I'm in and out of my mom's all the time and I see Frost if she's staying. I thought she liked me. Sometimes I've even thrown the ball for her down at the pond. To give Maud a chance to rest her arm. That dog doesn't tire easily."

I gestured to Keats. "Neither does her brother. Any idea why she was so agitated yesterday?"

Sunny shook her head. "Zoe said maybe the dog was in heat but I sure hope not because Maud would have a heart attack if Frost met up with the wrong male."

"If Frost was looking for love in all the wrong places, the library wouldn't be a likely stop." I frowned, trying to think of a logical explanation. "Or am I missing something?"

"I assumed she was just fed up from being on the run by then. She looked beat. But I was the one who got a beatdown."

"Like she didn't recognize you?" I said.

"More like she was waiting for someone," Sunny said. "And it wasn't me."

"Ah! Maud, I suppose. But why not just go home? It's not a big town so she must know the way."

Jilly ran her finger along the glass and inspected the cheeses on display. Even in the middle of an investigation, the chef was just below the surface. "It sounds like Frost was disoriented. Beside herself."

"Well, it wasn't my mom's fault, if that's what you're thinking." Sunny started sticking toothpicks into cubes of white cheese. "She's never had a problem with Frost before. Otherwise, Maud wouldn't have left her there."

I jacked up my smile a couple of notches. "Maud trusted your mom for good reason. It sounds like Frost went a little nuts yesterday."

Coming around the counter, Sunny offered a tray of samples. "Try some cheese." Jilly and I shook our heads but she practically shoved the platter into my midriff. "My boss is watching. If you don't look like you're about to buy a pound of smoked gouda, we'll all get tossed out of here. I'm not in her good books right now."

Jilly pulled out her wallet. "I'll take half a pound of smoked gouda. And another half of your finest stilton. It's the least we can do for Maud."

Sunny went back to her post. "Maud prefers soft cheese. I'll get her favorites."

As she packaged our hostess gift, Percy scaled my back and leaned down from my shoulder to poke a paw into my front pocket. He managed to catch the rubber backing on my phone with a claw and started to drag it out. I took the second phone hint of the day and when Sunny joined us again with two packages wrapped in brown paper, I asked, "Do you happen to have a picture of Frost at your mom's place? After you got her home."

She pulled her phone from her back pocket. "Yeah. Although we shouldn't have to prove ourselves like criminals."

"No one's suggesting that," Jilly said, as we peered at the screen. "It might give Maud peace of mind to know she made it back safely."

"And help us put a chronology together," I said. "It looks like you arrived home by three."

Sunny pointed to a photo of a nice spread of cheese on Darnese's counter beside the red tin of dog kibble. "Stayed for dinner because Mom was stressed like you wouldn't believe. She's getting a little tired of cheese but I get a good discount."

There was another photo of Frost after that. She was lying near the front door looking utterly dejected. It sent a bolt of pain into my heart. What had troubled that dog so much?

"She looks sad," Jilly said, as I used my phone to snap a photo of Sunny's screen. "Did you stay the night?"

"I offered to, but Mom said she was good. We leashed Frost and took her out together and it went fine. The dog had given up by then."

"Sure looks that way." I swiped the screen quickly to get a look at the rest of Sunny's collection, and snapped more photos. "Any idea how someone managed to sneak in and take the dog and her kibble?"

She shook her head, dispelling the last remnants of sullenness. Her fondness for both the dog and Darnese had softened her features better than a good head of hair. "I really can't understand it. I'm the only one with a key to the house because Mom's always worried about... well, trouble."

"She told us about your brother," I said. "Kale, right?"

Grabbing her phone from me, she went back around the counter to spear more cheese cubes with toothpicks. "He's doing better. Got a job that pays well."

"It's great that you keep in touch," I said. "I drifted away from my brother and sisters for ten years and we nearly ended up strangers."

"Kale's not a bad guy," she said, stabbing the cubes with unnecessary force. "Got in with the wrong crowd, that's all."

"The right crowd is everything," Jilly said. "Our friends keep us on track in a way our parents can't. Ivy and her crew are my family now."

Keats nudged my leg and mumbled a prompt. "Was that Kale in your photos?" I asked. "He looks very fit."

I'd noticed several shots of a man wearing a rusty orange baseball cap. From the brilliant leaves and scenery, it looked like they'd been hiking in the hills just weeks ago.

All the photos caught the man from behind. Maybe her brother didn't want his picture taken in case their mom got angry they were hanging out. Or maybe Kale wasn't doing as well as Sunny let on.

Either way, Sunny closed the information shop up tight. Her dark eyes grew cold and she slapped on a big smile that looked about as sincere as my HR versions felt.

"Enjoy that camembert, ma'ams," she said. "I'm sure your taste for cheese will come back when the dog does."

CHAPTER FIFTEEN

The Thistledown Public Library was absolutely adorable. Anyone would agree, although I couldn't deny having a weakness for libraries in any shape or form. I visited many while driving around hill country, but never had I found one set up in an original schoolhouse. The building had a fresh coat of red paint and window boxes full of flowers. The blooms were artificial but decidedly upscale fall fakery. The bell on the porch was likely a replica, too, but from where I stood on the front walk, it looked real.

Maybe diverting funds from policing to decoration wasn't such a bad idea.

Jilly would have loved the place, but she'd decided to head back to the Gentry house to deliver the cheese and update Maud on what we'd learned so far. Hopefully we could swing by here after a successful resolution to our puzzle.

It was probably just as well I'd come with only the dog and cat as backup. My conversations with Dottie Bridges, our long-time librarian in Clover Grove, always gave my brain a good workout and no friend of hers could be a pushover. However, with the grapevine being a bit slow around here, there was a chance she was behind on my latest exploits. Surely two librarians had more to talk about than a hobby farmer with an audacious side hustle.

Keats gave a mumble that told me not to get cocky, but he was plenty cocky for both of us. Percy flicked his tail as he swaggered up the ramp, seemingly certain that the librarian would fall for his charms. It was a stereotype that all bookish people loved cats, but I was glad both animals felt good about the visit. I'd left home today feeling optimistic about our chances of finding Frost before nightfall but we hadn't made much progress. In fact, the story of her disappearance grew more muddled with every person we encountered.

I set one boot on the ramp, then stopped. An old woman was now blocking the open doorway to the schoolhouse, arms crossed over a prim powder-blue twinset. Her hair had been curled with rollers, and half-moon spectacles sat on the end of her nose. Staring over them, Thistledown's librarian checked me out from ponytail to boots and frowned. Perhaps, like Elmer Mogus, Thelma Tilrow preferred women to dress like women. In her case, that meant a tweed skirt, thick hose and sensible Oxfords. One day that could happen to me, but I was more likely to end up in camouflage or a poncho.

"Hi there," I said, hauling out my very best HR smile. I already knew it was inadequate for the job but I had to give it a shot. "I've heard great things about you, Miss Tilrow. I'm Ivy—"

"Obviously." She flicked dismissive fingertips at me and then recrossed her arms. "I knew about you even before Dottie Bridges told me. I started your file over a year ago."

I didn't bother taking another step. Clearly I'd need to win my way across the drawbridge and into the fortress. "A file? Why?"

Her pucker was reminiscent of Dottie's. Perhaps there was a pucker class in librarian school, along with mandatory hushing and disapproving clucks. I'd been on the receiving end of all of these, despite being an ideal patron. I was the nerdy girl who got excited when books I ordered came in. The girl who hung out in the romantic poetry aisle. The girl who only dated books until Kellan came along.

Fifteen years later, my stellar bookish record was probably erased when I started traveling with a pack of animals and researching murders.

"I was afraid you'd turn up here one day," Thelma said. "It appears my fears were justified."

Somehow, I found a little more juice for my smile. "I love libraries. Did Dottie tell you I learned the Dewey decimal system by fourth grade and always filed books exactly where I found them? And that she tried to hire me?"

Her pucker released and I took pride in surprising her so soon. "As what, exactly?"

"As a page. Shelving books. She said I spent so much time cleaning up after my classmates I might as well get paid for it."

"And you turned her down? Jobs must have been hard to find in Clover Grove."

"I always believed the best jobs were those you'd do for free. Joining the payroll would have ruined it for me." I shrugged. "I admit there was a long stretch where my priorities were derailed. My head's on straight again."

"I see. So, running a farm is something you'd do for free."

"Oh, yes. And even pay for the privilege."

The pucker returned. "What about everything else on your file? I'm sure you know the highlights."

"Same. I wouldn't pay to get my butt kicked by criminals, but I'm okay with doing it for the sheer satisfaction of doing the right thing."

One of her hands lifted to touch a sausage curl that looked shellacked in place. "I thought Dottie was exaggerating, but you are a strange girl. Did you really take a horse into her stacks?"

"Just a miniature horse. As well as a donkey. They were helping me solve a case, but it was Dottie who cracked it."

Her half-moon glasses slipped right off her nose and dangled by a silver chain. "I thought she was exaggerating about that, too. Dottie and I have always had a friendly rivalry. We challenge each other to find the best research on any given subject."

I dared to take another step up the ramp. "Then perhaps I could engage you in a challenge today. You'd have a story to tell Dottie."

She crossed her arms again. "Has there been a murder in Thistledown I don't know about?"

"A murder, no." Beside me, Keats offered a mumble that gave me pause. "Not that I know of, anyway. But a dog's gone missing under suspicious circumstances and you could help bring her home."

"I have no idea where Maud Gentry's dog has gone." She set her glasses back on her nose. "That woman isn't welcome here until she returns my purloined essays by E.B. White. The book is months overdue."

"I love his work myself," I said. "He wrote so well about dogs. But this isn't really about Maud. It's about Frost. Roberta Frost. And you like dogs."

She pulled a disapproving sniff out of her librarian arsenal. "Why would you say so?"

"Because my dog likes you, and he hasn't been too impressed with anyone else around here. He's quite discriminating."

Keats fanned his tail and confirmed the truth of my words with a mumble. He did like Thelma Tilrow and he thought she knew more than she was letting on.

"I'm unmoved by your flattery, Ivy. If I give you an inch you'll take a mile. Dogs are not permitted inside."

"Hope that rule doesn't apply to cats," I said, "because Percy Bysshe Shelley is already inside taking a look around."

She turned instantly and I rushed up the ramp and caught the door before she could pull it closed.

"My sheepdog, John Keats, is very well trained," I said, when we were inside.

"Oh, stop pelting me with poets." She sounded exasperated. "I suppose you think that will impress me."

I grinned at her. "I have another dog named Lord Byron and so many more opportunities to keep the great writers alive. Sometimes when I'm turning manure, I recite my favorite poetry."

"Stop that foolishness. You're trying to fluster me and I assure you, Dottie is a far easier mark."

"To be fair, having a mini horse and donkey in the stacks would fluster most librarians," I said. "Dottie's awesome."

Percy was sitting on the front desk, with his tail wrapped neatly around his paws.

"Off." Thelma picked up a newspaper and fanned it at him. "Shoo."

Instead, Percy moved into pounce position and I quickly stepped in front of the older woman. He landed on my shoulder and swished his tail in front of my eyes as I turned to face her.

"I thought all book people liked cats," I said, letting his fluff hide my smirk.

"A stereotype," she said, moving around the desk and perching on a stool with casters. "As you said, I'm more of a dog person, although they're unwelcome in my library."

Keats sniffed around the desk and went into a point beside her. There was a small tuft of brown and white fur on the industrial gray carpet.

"Frost was in your library yesterday," I said, gesturing to the fur. "Why not her brother?"

Her sharp intake of breath wasn't in the usual librarian catalogue of sounds. I had won a point. Perhaps even impressed her a little. "Well, I couldn't just leave her sitting out there, could I? She was parked at the bottom of the ramp with that little boot on. Wendel Barrick nearly tripped over her and could have broken a hip. I have no idea why she turned up here."

I perched on the edge of her desk, putting her pucker back in place. "You do know why. Frost came here—and stayed here—because she trusted you, Miss Tilrow. It's the only place she didn't bolt from, apparently."

Thelma looked somewhat gratified. "I wanted to call Darnese Bibb but she wouldn't have it."

"Frost wouldn't? How did you know?"

A little color rose in her cheeks. "That dog mumbled away like it was children's story hour. I knew Maud was out of town and when I mentioned Darnese, Frost's tone got a bit heated. She's a very expressive dog."

"Huh." I looked down at Keats. "I guess some things run in the family. He has plenty to say, too."

He mumbled a retort that won him a strange look from Thelma. "Indeed," the old woman said. "I don't speak canine but I did what I could. I put Frost in my office to rest for an hour or so. When I came to collect her, she'd gone. The back door was open and I suppose she let herself out."

"She's good with doorknobs, I hear. Any idea where she went next?"

Thelma shook her head and sighed. "I wouldn't say this to just anyone, Ivy, but I do believe that dog was trying to tell me something. Frost was clearly in some distress and I would have liked to help more. I planned to take her home with me until

Maud got back. Then I could have struck a bargain and exchanged the dog for E.B. White."

The merest trace of a smile told me it was a joke.

"It was good of you to be so kind to Frost. By all accounts, she was quite stressed. Someone said it was like she was under attack."

The librarian scooted back on the stool and patted her stiff curls with both hands. "I got the same impression. I wondered if someone took advantage of Maud's absence to move in for the—well, dognapping."

Keats poked me in the leg and I cut to the chase. "Miss Tilrow, librarians always know what's going on in a community. Dottie Bridges is probably the most observant woman I've ever met. If you're good friends—"

"Best friends. We're cut from the same cloth."

"Then I bet you have a good idea who might want to part Maud from her dog."

Rolling back and forth over the plastic behind her desk, she puckered and pondered. Finally, she said, "Librarians have a code of ethics, young lady. We can't just splatter wild speculation around. No one would trust us."

"The dog trusted you. And I suspect you trust me. I come with good references."

"And a very thick file." She jerked her thumb over her shoulder at a stand holding a few folders. "This isn't even your town. You won't care if you damage the reputation I've worked decades to build."

"I *will* care because Dottie and I are friends now, at least from where I stand. So please, give me a hint if you can. Anything that might help me reunite that dog with her family."

Thelma closed her eyes, still patting curls that never moved. "Try June Lunde," she said, at last. "Perhaps she knows something."

I pulled out my phone and googled quickly. My mouth opened and a gasp fell out. "June Lunde, the breeder of prize-winning border collies? Do you think she stole Frost?"

"I would never presume such. Not when June's record of book returns is spotless." She unbuttoned and rebuttoned her blue cardigan. "All I can say is that more people should remember to clear their browser history." She gestured toward the big computers that looked a decade old. "I always check. For their own protection."

I got up as quickly as I could without dislodging Percy from my shoulder. "June was researching Maud Gentry and Frost?"

She covered her mouth and coughed. Behind the fingertip shield she whispered, "And *you*. Dottie would want you to know that. So, do be careful, Ivy."

"I always am," I said, hurrying to the door.

"I have a fat file that says otherwise," she called after me. "But you're welcome to prove your claims about shelving books. The romantic poets could use an audit."

After letting the pets out, I turned and saluted. "When Frost is home safe, Thelma... game on!"

CHAPTER SIXTEEN

Maud Gentry flushed an unhealthy shade of puce when I told her the news. "June Lunde stole my dog? That's —that's—"

"Unthinkable," Louisa said. "Despicable."

She plucked some twigs out of her hair and snapped them angrily. The trails had taken quite a toll on Lou, apparently, because Gertie and Edna had sent her home in a cab and continued on their own.

"It's just a lead," I said. "Not a fact. She's been in the library researching you, that's all."

And me, which was weird, but there was no reason to cause further alarm. Not yet, anyway.

Maud paced back and forth in her small kitchen. Her life might be in disarray but her house was not. While we were all trying to track down the dog, she had been cleaning. There were sponges and rubber gloves and bottles of disinfectant in every room.

"Why would June need to research me?" she asked. "We've spoken a dozen times. Met in person twice."

"You never told me that," Lou said. "What did she want?"

"Frost, obviously," her aunt said. "She offered me a ridiculous sum. No dog is worth that kind of money." She looked down at Keats and found a little smile. "Present company excepted."

He mumbled agreement and her smile got stronger.

"I would think Frost is worth plenty, considering she can be bred," I said.

Maud picked up a shammy and started buffing the counter. The nervous habit reminded me of my clean-freak sister, Daisy. "Frost is worth a lot but not the kind of money June was throwing around. I can't imagine where she got it. Breeding dogs is no way to get rich, at least on a small scale."

"Maybe she inherited money," Jilly said.

"Or robbed a bank," Lou suggested. "But even if she had the coin, why splurge on one dog?"

"Didn't ask. Just turned her down flat." Maud buffed harder. "So, then she tried to put down a huge deposit for a couple of Frost's puppies. Females she could eventually breed."

"Is Frost pregnant?" I asked. "The vet technician speculated she was in heat."

Maud shook her head. "I haven't found a sire worthy of her, including June's stud. I won't breed her until I can. Frost has been through heat twice and I kept her on a very tight leash."

"Isn't there such a thing as a silent heat?" I asked. "Google says so."

"It wouldn't be silent to an experienced breeder like me." The shammy slowed, possibly signifying slight doubt. "Certainly no one else could tell if I can't."

"Not June Lunde?" I asked. "What if June Lunde stole Frost from Darnese's house so that nature could take its course with her stud?"

Now she twisted the shammy with both hands. "I'd wring her neck. Skip's bloodlines are all wrong. You can't just throw two dogs together and manifest champions. I looked high and low before creating magic with Keats, and then Frost."

"I bet she stole Frost," Lou said. "June would at least have the decency to take the kibble. She'd know you can't change a dog's food suddenly."

"But there have been a couple reports of sightings today," Maud said. "Unsubstantiated, though. I don't know what to believe anymore."

"She could have escaped again," Jilly suggested. "Frost sounds like a furry Houdini."

I put my coat back on. "When you don't know what to believe all you can do is follow the leads and see where they take you. If Frost has been anywhere in the vicinity of the Lunde house, Keats will know."

"I'm coming with you," Maud said, dropping the shammy. "If June stole my dog, I'll borrow your friend's rifle and—"

"Gertie's gun isn't that cooperative," I said. "Slippery as an eel."

Maud gave me a glacial stare. "I've fired a rifle, Ivy. You should learn how, too."

"That's a skill I'd like to master," Lou said. "It doesn't feel safe around here anymore."

"Best to start a little smaller," her aunt said. "If you climbed a tree to escape unarmed women, you probably aren't ready for a rifle."

"We're not, either," I told Lou, as Keats nudged me from behind to get going. "Weapons are more likely to be turned against us. According to Edna and Gertie."

After smoothing her hair, Maud plucked her coat off a hook near the door. Behind her back, Jilly and I exchanged a glance, and my friend stepped into the breach.

"Wouldn't it be better if you waited here for Frost, Maud?" she said. "In case she's on the run again?"

Maud shoved an arm into the wrong sleeve. "I need to speak to June directly. Breeder to breeder. You girls won't know if she's telling the truth."

"We will," I said. "Keats will. Percy will. Jilly and I know how to read people, and the pets do the rest."

Maud leveled a stare at me. "Then I want to see this in action."

"That's just it," Jilly said. "With more variables, there's more to go wrong."

"Auntie," Lou said. "They don't want you distracting Keats as he works."

"I know how to handle myself," Maud said, trying to force the other arm into the wrong sleeve. "I've been working with dogs my entire life."

"No one is questioning that," I said. "But just the slightest shift in energy can throw us off our game. Keats might be distracted if you're there. He probably wants to impress you, but this isn't the time."

Keats gave an annoyed grumble, perhaps reminding me he'd kept his composure through much worse. He never lost focus with killers, but I suspected he underestimated just how distracting family could be. Maud, Louisa and Frost were exactly that—his family. Negotiating relationships new and old would be an adjustment for all of us.

Louisa had seemed somewhat intimidated by her aunt, but she stepped forward to untangle the coat that was rapidly turning into a trap. "Aunt Maud, please. Just let Ivy and her crew do their thing. That's why you asked me to go and find them."

I understood the look in Maud's eyes as they darted around the room. To stand by and do nothing when her dog was in danger was torture. It required a leap of faith from someone who probably had very little of that left. She'd lost two precious dogs before and this time the grief would be cumulative and potentially overwhelming.

"We've got this, Maud," I said. "You can trust us."

She let the coat drop into Lou's hands. "I don't trust anyone. How could I, after what's happened? Please take Louisa, at least."

"Louisa, but not Fanny," I said. "Unless you can rein her in. Percy needs to focus, too, and she's pestering him."

Lou raised her eyebrows. "Pestering him? She's just sitting there."

Poor Percy was shut in the powder room for Fanny's safety, and the gray cat had her nose to the crack underneath. She wasn't growling, but I knew the language of cats, and this was a subtle provocation.

"Lou, you're in denial about your cat," I said. "That never serves anyone. Deal with her so that Percy can come out. We've got to hit the road before it gets dark."

I was asking a lot of the sun, because it set so early in November, but it honestly seemed to be doing its best for us, dropping ever more slowly to the horizon.

"I hope June has the dog," Jilly said as we followed Lou's directions to the breeder's home. Keats had his nose out the open window, sniffing for the sister he'd never met. "I would hate for Frost to be on her own in the bush overnight."

Lou leaned forward between the seats, pointing left when I'd already put the signal on. A backseat driver I didn't need with two good navigators up front.

"She'd find a place to hole up," Lou said. "Frost is brilliant. So brilliant that what's happening makes no sense at all."

I made the turn and gestured for Lou to lean back. "If she's anything like her brother, it probably makes complete sense to her."

"Unless she's overcome by hormones," Jilly said.

Keats didn't pull his head in but since my hand was on his side, I got the gist of his mumble. No sister of his would be letting her hormones exclusively run the show.

"Easy to say when you don't have those hormones driving you," Jilly added, laughing. "It's not easy having a ticking clock."

I laughed, too. "It certainly isn't."

After a moment, Lou spoke from the back seat. "You both understand this dog when he mumbles like that?"

Jilly and I shrugged in unison. "We don't always know what we know or how we know it," I said. "But our profession trained us to read people—every nuance of communication, spoken or otherwise. Over time, we've come to know enough about what Keats means and he gets better and better at driving his point home."

Turning to glance into the back seat, Jilly smiled. "I bet you have a good idea about what Fanny wants, whether you know it or not. You two seem to have a strong connection."

The pretty gray cat was in a crate on Lou's lap. She burst into a loud purr as if to confirm Jilly's supposition. "What's Fanny telling you right now?" I asked.

"That you're right," Louisa said. "And that she'd be enjoying all this if not for—"

Percy's little hiss from Jilly's lap cut her off. The animosity between them had settled considerably since I took my cat's side but I'd still need to monitor him closely.

"Don't waste your breath, Percy," I said. "We'll need all of our focus and energy to get to the bottom of this. You and Fanny can sort things out later, when Frost is home."

A pair of huffy cat sounds collided overhead and we all laughed.

"I understood that," Lou said. "Maybe I've been picking up more than I know."

"Guaranteed." I turned into a lane beside a sign that said,

"Lunde's Premium Border Collies."

Keats pulled his head in with a snort of what seemed like disgust. What June was breeding here wasn't stellar quality as far as his nose was concerned.

The breeder came out on the porch as we pulled right up to the house. She was about Maud's age but looked older, with wiry gray hair and deep creases framing her eyes. Time and worry had likely taken a toll on her, too. I was beginning to recognize the signs and wondered if they also showed on my face. Would I look old enough to be my child's grandmother when I finally welcomed a new addition to the family?

Lou was the first to jump out of the truck. "Hi, June. This is—"

"I know who they are," June said, staring as Jilly and I joined Louisa. The breeder's eyes fell to Keats, whose ears were under my fingertips. "And I know that dog."

I, in turn, knew the look in her eyes. It was hungry. Desperate, even. I'd seen it on the Langman sisters when they looked at a valuable antique, and more recently, when a professor and parrot collector had tried to get his claws on Hannah Pemberton's African gray, Duncan. They were like addicts in need of a fix.

That look made me want to load my dog back into the truck and lock the doors. But June had already shown her weakness. There was no need for me to expose mine.

"Miss Lunde, we're here about Frost, Maud Gentry's dog," I said. "As you may have heard, she's gone missing and we thought she might have escaped and turned up here."

June crossed her arms. She was wearing a heavy fleece-lined cardigan over a sweatsuit and slippers. "Why would she come here? It's a long journey from town, although I won't deny I'd be happy to see her."

Lou started to speak, then stopped, likely because Jilly was employing the same arm pinch she used to choke off my words. With Percy strutting up the front stairs, my friend's hands were free to control the verbal traffic flow.

"There's been some suggestion that the dog is in heat," I said. "And I understand you have an available sire."

"I do, actually. Skip's in his run out back."

We followed her around the side of the house and my heart sank when I saw she'd applied the word "run" to a small cement yard surrounded by metal bars. The border collie may well have passed for Keats, given the similarity in their markings, but that's where the resemblance ended. Skip's posture seemed slumped and his brown eyes listless. He took all of us in at a glance and retreated to the far side of the pen.

I pressed my lips together, knowing it wasn't my place to judge how others handled their pets. The words came out in spite of me. "You keep your border collie in a cage?"

"This is not a cage." June's tone was defensive. "His run exceeds industry standards by far."

"Why confine him at all? He's a border collie. Being trapped like that must be—"

Jilly's fingers found my forearm and pinched off the rest of my sentence. "Ms. Lunde, you'll need to excuse us," she said. "Sometimes we forget how lucky we are to live on a farm, the sheepdog's natural environment."

Keats mumbled something that sounded both assertive and pitying. It must have made June uncomfortable because she stepped away from him.

"Skip is perfectly happy with his life here, and yes, I'd appreciate it if you didn't project your reformed city girl notions onto him. He's not a child. He's breeding stock."

Hearing Skip reduced to mere breeding stock was disappointing, to say the least. No wonder Maud would have nothing to do with her. Frost lived a good life and was prized for far more than her genes. There was no way Maud would relegate any pups to a situation like this. Skip looked healthy, but sheepdogs needed more than a couple of square meals and a pen to thrive. They needed to work hard and pretty much constantly. No matter what jobs I asked of Keats, he was always ready for more challenge.

After a moment, I managed to retrieve an HR smile, if only because Lou was observing me closely. "You're right," I said. "We do bring our preconceptions. I apologize." I flicked my fingers for Keats and Percy to fan out. "I understand you've been in discussions with Maud about Frost."

June moved in front of me in an apparent attempt to block Skip from my view. "And was summarily shut down. I hope you're not suggesting I had anything to do with her disappearance."

"Not at all," Jilly said. "We were just curious about whether Frost may have ended up here. Witnesses say she was an escape artist and also quite agitated. Perhaps she considered you and Skip to be a safe haven."

The creases around June's eyes eased a little. "I'm not the only one who'd appreciate access to Frost's bloodlines and I was willing to take out a reverse mortgage to pull it off. But no breeder with any common sense would bother to try without Maud's approval. Whatever you think of my Skip, he's a pedigreed dog, and his offspring could only get their papers with a legitimate pairing."

"Unless Frost just happened to be in the right place at the right time," Lou said.

Crossing her arms again, June glared at Lou. "I won't deny that would make me extremely happy, but I don't see any sign of her. Do you?"

All of us shook our heads. I didn't see any sign of another dog, but more importantly, Keats didn't, either. He'd done a quick sweep of the area and come up empty. Percy trotted around the side of the house looking disgruntled, too. Had we wasted valuable hours of daylight on a false lead? I was so sure Thelma Tilrow had put us on course.

Keats' blue eye caught me in its eerie glow and he mumbled a suggestion to press on with the conversation. Maybe it wasn't entirely a bust after all.

"Ms. Lunde, if you don't mind my asking, where are the rest of your dogs? A breeding program with only one male must be doomed to failure."

A muffled snort told me Jilly's fingers were at work on Lou again.

June scuffed the dry soil with her slipper and stared over my shoulder. "I had two dams but they disappeared a while back. The first I assumed was an accident—that perhaps coyotes had nabbed her. The second vanished from this very yard when there was only a fence. That's why Skip is confined to quarters. He still likes being outside but I can't leave anything more to chance."

The judgment I'd felt for her earlier washed away instantly. Yes, Skip was probably miserable being denied his birthright as a sheepdog, but it came from her fear of losing him.

"That can't be a coincidence," I said. "Or are other dogs disappearing from this area, too?"

She shook her head. "As far as I know, only my dogs went missing. Until Frost." Hugging herself, she added, "I am sorry if that's what happened to Maud. Losing my girls broke my spirit. It's only started to come back recently. I thought perhaps it was safe to try again."

The hunger I saw in her eyes earlier wasn't quite what I'd thought, either. This was an important reminder to keep an open mind, especially when I felt passionate about something.

"I'm sorry about what happened," I said. "Are there other

breeders in the area we should check in with?"

"Very few locals have border collies," she said. "None are breeding dogs."

Keats nudged my shin to tell me to wrap things up. I took down the names of the other owners. Then I offered my hand to June and she squeezed my fingers far too hard.

"I hope you get a chance to try again," I said. "And that you can find a safe way to give Skip more freedom."

The dog's sad eyes lifted to mine and he gave a little whine.

June glanced at him. "Perhaps, if this business around Frost turns out to be nothing serious. Seeing your dog live his best life has reminded me of what Skip is sacrificing for safety." She walked us back around the house. "It's a shame you had Keats neutered."

I held my fingers to my lips. "He didn't really realize what he lost till we came here. No need to rub salt in the wound."

She smiled and the eye creases somehow deepened and eased at the same time. "I guess it's left him freer to help in your work. He only has one job to do."

Keats gave an indignant mumble and I translated. "He has lots of jobs to do. Reproducing doesn't happen to be one of them."

"Good luck finding Frost," she said. "I wanted to join the search party, but your friends scared me."

I laughed as I followed the others into the truck. "They'll be proud to hear that."

"Please come out in the morning, June," Lou said. "By that time we'll need all hands on deck."

Keats gave another mumble as we drove off and I turned to him in surprise. It had sounded very much like, "Too late."

Too late for what? To find his sister?

I rested my hand on his sleek side but if he knew the answer to my silent query, he kept it to himself.

CHAPTER SEVENTEEN

Jilly offered to throw dinner together with whatever she found in the kitchen. I knew she'd turn it into something awesome, but it could take a while, especially with Louisa acting as sous chef. Edna and Gertie had texted to say they'd take care of their own dinner and I hoped that didn't include trapping or shooting any wildlife. They'd left some of their gear behind but were probably packing energy bars.

Keats mumbled a suggestion and I nodded. Maud turned away from the window, another shammy dangling from her hand. "What does he want?"

"To go for a walk," I said. "Where you usually take Frost. Sunny Bibb said she saw you down by the pond quite often."

A slight shudder ran over the breeder. "We won't find Frost there because she knows the area well and would just come home. But we'd likely run into other people. I can't bear pity and false reassurance. No one can possibly understand what this is like."

"June Lunde can," I said. "As can I, because I've lost animals I love. Regardless, Keats wants to go to the pond and would like you to come along."

His next mumble sounded cautiously optimistic, so I assumed there was something to be gained from a cold walk neither Maud nor I particularly wanted to take.

His breeder must have thought so too, because she went to get her coat. Before we left the house, I gently tugged the shammy out of her hand and she sighed. "The house has never been cleaner. I prefer it with a lived-in feel."

"It'll be covered with fur and paw prints again soon. My crew will do their part."

Keats and Percy led us into the backyard and onto a trail. I confirmed with a glance at Maud that this was her usual route.

She nodded. "Takes a little longer this way but less risk of running into Darnese or Elmer. Or the rest of the nosey parkers."

The sun was a fiery red ball ready to sink heavily into night but very little light penetrated the bush. As with everywhere else I'd been in hill country, the woods were dense and unwelcoming. At least, it felt that way to me. Keats' tail was high, white tuft nearly lighting the way for us, and Percy's orange fluff helped, too. I didn't need to turn on my phone light till the dog stopped at a fork in the trail.

"Which way?" I asked Maud.

"Turn right to the pond," she said. "The other trail leads to the meadows. Not safe this time of night."

"It sounds like you aren't safe period, Maud. Lou told us someone tried to run you down."

She gave a heavy sigh. "That was ages ago and probably nothing. I wish Lou hadn't moved here to watch over me like a mother hen. She's too young for that kind of sacrifice."

"That's what family does, I guess. Look out for each other."

"I'm careful. The biggest threat around here has been wild boars. We also have a pair of vagrants who camp out year round. Harmless, but they do startle me sometimes."

"A pair? As in a couple?" I asked. "Living in the bush?"

She nudged me between the shoulder blades to keep moving. "There are probably more people like that than you know. The disillusioned and disenfranchised. Some are in the bunkers your senior friends go on about. Others prefer to keep moving. Rickie and Madge Merriweather lost their old house a few years ago in a foreclosure. The locals wanted to come together to help but the couple preferred to make their own way in the world. They must be about seventy and it can't be easy even with the supplies some of us leave out for them."

The trail opened into a small park with an oval pond that glowed like an orange eye in the late-day rays.

"It's something I could see Edna doing," I said. "Selling her place and living a nomadic lifestyle. As long as she could visit her recliner in a shack now and then."

"Some days it sounds appealing. Warmer days, anyway." Maud stared around the park. "Frost and I come here almost every night. There's plenty of room for fetch and drills. As you know, it takes work to wear out these dogs."

"Definitely. Keats has no interest in fetch, though."

Her eyes dropped to my dog and a smile flickered on and then off. It was like a lightbulb that had come a bit loose. "He never did. That's why I worked on tricks with him. He was like a circus dog."

"His tricks are what compelled me to rescue him from Skint. The murderer. When I visited the guy's yard, Keats would go through an elaborate repertoire without any prompting from me. I knew he was a genius in the wrong hands."

"Then I'm so glad I did the work," she said. "On the whole, I'm not a fan of tricks or fetch, but you need to find the motivator for each dog. It's like a key in the lock of the pup's mind.

After that, they seem able to take in anything you throw at them. It instils a love of learning."

"It worked beautifully. I couldn't imagine a dog more driven to learn than Keats. What was the key for Frost? Fetch or drills?"

"Neither. Those were just slumming for her. What she loved most was scent work. I'd hide her favorite stuffed toys around the house and call them out by name—horse, pig, lemur and so on. She'd find them one by one. Later, we expanded to the yard and sometimes even the woods. That's what turned her crank, and once it's turning, nothing can stop the right dog." Her eyes lifted from Keats. "As you know."

I gestured to a bench and she joined me. "I always wondered how he became the Einstein of sheepdogs. Sounds like it all started with circus tricks."

Perching on the edge of the wooden bench, she shook her head. "Started well before that. Decades, in fact. I hand-picked every single one of his ancestors, right back to the dogs I found in the English countryside. There was no such thing as email, then, let alone websites with family trees. It was all about word of mouth and references, with a healthy dose of intuition. But I was never satisfied until I met the dogs and their owners. We all had to be on the same wavelength. When I found a gem, a little bell rang in my head. Over the years, I bought a dozen dogs from an eccentric woman who lived on the moors. Could barely understand a word she said but when it came to dogs, we spoke the same language. She wouldn't sell to many, but she trusted me. A chap in Wales sold me a few and another man on the Isle of Skye a few more. Between them, I got enough diversity for strong lines. All told, I invested thousands—tens of thousands, if I'm honest—in genetic and other testing. With every generation it distilled to the essence you see before you. This was my life's work."

"And now there's just Frost?" I said.

Her eyes shifted away. "Just Frost. When I lost their mother, and their sire passed of natural causes, I decided to end my breeding program. I placed my remaining dogs in pet homes. Farms, mostly, where they have good lives. Of all my dogs, only Keats is living to his true potential."

He gave a humblebrag that garnered Maud's brightest smile yet. It was very attractive, and for the first time I saw the resemblance, beyond blue eyes, between her and Louisa.

"I didn't dare work Frost any harder than necessary to stimulate her mind," she continued. "She may very well have been the brightest of them all but the last thing I wanted to do was attract attention to her."

"What happened to their mother?" I asked.

"Same as Keats, pretty much," she said. "I thought what happened with him was a fluke, so I went to a national agility trial with Anne, his dam. Agility was her great passion and it had taken us around the country. She won first that day and when I left her with a caretaker and went to grab a bite, someone stole her. Crate and all. No one saw a thing, apparently. The police had no interest in the disappearance, just like now."

The smile flickered out again, and tears began streaming down her face as she stared out at the water.

"How long ago was that?" I asked, letting Percy jump into my lap and hugging him close. As always, his purr warmed me from the inside out.

"Just over a year. That's when I moved here." She rubbed her cheeks with a woolen glove. "My Annie had two blue eyes that glowed out of her black face. Never saw a more striking dog. Keats takes after her, and Frost their sire."

"She may still be alive," I said. "Anne."

"Possibly. But I searched high and low and can't imagine I'll see her again." She continued to chafe at her cheeks and I turned away to give her a moment. Eventually, she continued. "I named her after the Brontë that never got the attention she deserved because of her flashier sisters."

"Aha! So you lied about the literary allusions."

It was the first time I'd heard Maud laugh. "It doesn't pay to have pretensions in hill country. People already wanted to take me down a notch. At any rate, I did it to honor the eccentric breeder on the moors. She started the trend." Turning to me she raised her eyebrows, as delicate as silver swallows. "What I want to know is how you decided on the name Keats."

I blinked at her a few times, suddenly aware of moisture beading my own lashes. Hearing about Keats' lost mother had moved me, too. "It was his name. Or the closest I could get to it at the time."

Her eyes were fixed on me. "Are you a psychic or something?"

"Just a regular HR exec turned farmer, who happens to like poetry. If anyone's a psychic, it's the dog. It seemed like that was what he was telling me."

Keats mumbled something and his breeder laughed again. "I can see how you might mistake the first letter and get the wrong poet. Used to irk me to no end when dog show judges pronounced it 'Yeets' instead of 'Yates.' So maybe it was for the best."

She reached down and touched his ears, sending a flare of irrational jealousy through me. Those ears had belonged to her once but they were mine now. They had to be, because I would be nothing without him.

Keats mumbled something to me. It sounded like assurance that I would be something all right, just not quite what we were together. We were greater than the sum of our parts, but individually we were amazing, too. If that's what he meant, I didn't want to think about it. His mouth fell open in a pant-laugh, plainly telling me I was being silly. There was no need for speculation because we were an inseparable team.

"I wanted this one for myself," Maud said, "but it wasn't meant to be. That's happened a few times over the years. I had to let dogs go to someone else. Their person. I never held them back from what they perceived as their destiny. However, I normally got some choice in the matter. This time fate took over."

The waves of jealousy and panic abated. She'd either found me worthy of the dog or respected the dog's decision. Either way, it didn't seem like she objected to our union.

"So there are other dogs as remarkable as Keats around?" I asked.

"A few, yes. I put the same care into every litter, and then focused even more on Annie's. All turned out to be good dogs, and some very good. Only a handful were great, and when it turned out their place wasn't with me, it was always heartbreaking. That's why I was so relieved Frost chose me. Many people offered, but again and again she decided to stay. Until apparently that choice was taken from her."

The sun had nearly dropped from sight but there was enough light to see the gleam in Keats' blue eye. He moved out from under his breeder's hand and gave her knee a poke and offered another mumble. There was a stern note in it.

"He's telling us it's time to go," she said.

"I beg to differ. He's telling you the game's not over. You can't throw in the shammy quite yet."

She groaned as she pushed herself upright with two palms on the bench. "I don't sense Frost out there. It's the first time I can't."

Her comment made me shiver. The thought of losing the mysterious connection to Keats was terrifying. "Maybe you can't, but Keats can. Who are you going to trust? Yourself or this dog you bred and trained with such care?"

The dog himself added some assertive mumbles to underscore my comment and prodded her to the trail. I would have preferred to take the road back to Maud's, but Keats had decided.

"I guess I trust the dog," she said. "I don't suppose you'd consider changing his name back to Yeats? That's what's on his paperwork."

I laughed as I turned on my phone light again. "I don't need paperwork to tell me this dog is best in breed. Turns out you chose the wrong poet, that's all."

There was a snort behind me as she followed me back down the trail. "Yeats, my boy, there is no accounting for taste."

CHAPTER EIGHTEEN

M y phone rang as we got back and I decided to take the call outside. Maud's house felt small compared to the inn and I appreciated an excuse to walk around, even if it came with a side order of stress.

Pressing speaker, I said, "Hey, Mom. What's up?"

"Darling, I'm about to deploy. That's what's up."

Her voice was so loud I turned the volume down and headed into the backyard. There was a small patio with just enough room to pace. A conversation with Mom was best accompanied by movement to keep tension from building.

"Deploy? What are you talking about? Big date tonight?"

Normally I didn't give her an opening to discuss her romantic activities, but her talk of rotational dating had diminished lately. She was splitting her energy between the salon and her sewing business. The demand for reconstituted secondhand clothing was growing faster than expected. By tamping down her flagrant use of scarlet and satin, Mom had found a few fashion-forward fans in larger communities, like Dorset Hills. It meant compromising her art but she was doing it with more ease than I thought possible.

"How could I even think about dating right now?" she said. "My youngest child is in crisis. I've been beside myself since Daisy told me."

It was a subtle jab over hearing the news indirectly but I let it pass. It was nothing a full circuit of the yard couldn't handle. Keats and Percy trotted in front of me, still in work mode. We all sensed this was just a break.

"Mom, I appreciate your concern but this isn't a crisis. At least, not compared to many situations I've faced. We're searching for a lost dog and I'm sure it won't be long before we find her."

"Ivy, I'm proud of you for putting up such a brave front when we both know this is about so much more than a lost dog."

It was always fascinating to hear how my mother's mind worked, and since I had a moment, I indulged her. "We do? What exactly do we know?"

"That woman has clearly concocted a fiction to steal our Keats. That's why I'm coming down to help. He's my favorite grandson and I won't allow it."

"Maud Gentry isn't trying to steal Keats. She just wants her own dog back."

"Darling, she has designs on our dog, you mark my words. You're far too gullible."

"Gullible? Jilly and I are known for being too cynical."

"Don't even mention Jillian to me right now. I'm too upset to talk about her."

Percy jumped onto the picnic table and then my shoulder, purring loudly. I hadn't planned to have this conversation till we were home but it seemed like the cat was telling me to go for it. He was firmly on Team Jilly.

Besides, it was easier to deal with Mom from a distance. With six kids, she'd long since mastered the art of controlling a room—usually with wild eyes, flailing hands and other histrionics. "Mom, if there's something you want to say about Jilly, you might as well spit it out. I'm alone right now."

There was a long pause at her end and I heard stilettos clicking over the hardwood floors. Jilly had asked her to wear slippers in the house but Mom didn't have the constitution for it. At barely five feet tall, she needed at least a kitten heel to feel on top of her world.

"Now's not the time. We'll talk about it when I have the situation contained."

"What situation could you possibly have with Jilly?"

She gave a huff of frustration. "The other situation. With the breeder and her niece. I'm coming down there to help find their dog and protect yours. I will put those two in their place."

A band of pressure tightened around my head, reminding me of the lurking migraine. Maybe now wasn't the time to engage Mom after all. I'd back out of this conversation and save my resources.

"Mom, you know how much I appreciate your support, but we've got the matter well in hand. We'll be searching rough and unfamiliar terrain."

"That's fine. I'm already packed and ready to roll."

"You're going to roll over unfamiliar terrain in satin pumps?"

"Oh, darling. I'm not a complete fool, as much as you kids like to suggest otherwise. I've packed my boots, but you can't expect me to drive in them. I need a nice heel. You know that."

"And you know you can't drive. Even if you could, Buttercup's on blocks."

"You just worry about guarding our dog from those Gentry grabbers and let me handle the commute."

"Our" dog paused and gave a pant-laugh. The wackier my mother got, the more he seemed to enjoy her.

"Mom, I need to hear exactly what you're planning so that I

know you're safe. And let's be honest, so that I know I'm safe from the wrath of my fiancé."

"Don't bring the chief into this. Although I'm sure he'd understand that family supports family. It's that simple."

"If you hit the road in a nice heel, Kellan will find out somehow. He always does. And right now he's got his hands full with an investigation. Just stay where you are, darling." I gasped in horror. "I mean, *Mom*. Oh my gosh."

She laughed and I couldn't help joining her.

"If you're laughing, I've exceeded my goals," she said.

I let out a sigh of relief. "You're not coming."

"Of course, we're coming. Your sisters will be here any minute to pick me up. The Galloway Girls will be out in full force, but I doubt Daisy will let me drive. She's as uptight as your intended."

"Okay, I've heard enough. Let me give Daisy a shout. I'll put all of you on standby for tomorrow, and only if needed."

There was a huffy sigh on her end. "Fine. See if I try to do anything nice again."

With that crisis averted, I circled back to the original one. "How about you save the positive energy for smoothing things over with Asher and Jilly?"

"There's nothing to smooth over. Although Asher was certainly in a snit this morning. He said I ran Jilly out of her own kitchen just because I made a few suggestions about organizing her spice drawer."

"Seriously? You don't even own spices. We grew up on a steady diet of bland. What's really going on?"

"Your brother is driving me crazy, that's what's going on. He leaves flecks of shaving foam on the mirror and bristles in the sink. He falls asleep on the couch and then complains about my heels waking him."

"He complains about your heels marking the floor because

it's important to Jilly that the inn looks great for guests. As for the bathroom, Daisy cleans it every single day, sometimes twice, and you have many other options. Again, what's really going on?"

"Living with men is impossible, that's all."

I stopped walking and gave this my full attention. We were on the verge of a breakthrough, I could feel it. "Mom, you lived with Asher till he was twenty-five and bought his own house. He was your golden boy and nothing much has changed in his personal grooming habits from what I can tell. Now you have your clean-freak daughter following behind him. So, one more time... What's really going on?"

I could feel her shiny, hard veneer cracking. "I liked it when it was just us. You and Jilly and me. That's when everything started coming together, you see. In my shoebox apartment I'd been living a small life. After moving in with you girls, I was finally able to grow. Thanks to you, I've started three businesses and never been happier. Except for Asher."

Keats poked my leg to get me moving again. Perhaps he knew pacing would help me walk this delicate tightrope.

"Mom, you really have grown but you don't need an inn to live a big life. You are the biggest tiny person I know. Jilly and I didn't do that for you. Far from it."

"You did. I was stunted. Locked in the perceptions others had of me." Her heels clicked faster. "I can't go back to being trapped like that. It was unbearable."

I did a full lap of the yard before answering. "Have you heard that Michelangelo quote? Something like, 'Every block of stone has a statue inside it and it's the task of the sculptor to discover it.'"

"Meaning what, exactly?"

"The way I see it, you're the sculptor of your own life and it won't change one bit with Asher around. You're just associating him with your old life and that's not fair because he's grown, too. We all have."

The clicking stopped. "I suppose I could get rubber tips on my shoes as I adapt. After all, Jilly doesn't wear heels at home anymore."

"That's right, now that I think of it."

"I'll never give them up for good because fashion is my business. Or one of them, thanks to you, Jilly and Michelangelo. Darling, you always know the right thing to say. I can't imagine where you got that skill because it wasn't from your father or me."

I laughed. "I appreciate the compliment, but if I give you the blame for all the negatives, you can have a share in the positives, too. That's family."

"Exactly. Family is there through thick and thin and I want to come down to help fend off that breeder. No one knows better than I do what Keats means to you. Since he came along, you've turned into a new person. I'd give the dog credit but according to Michelangelo, it's all coming from you."

I looked down at my dog and he gave a humblebrag.

"He's taking the credit on this one," I said. "We'll talk again tomorrow. For now, go and enjoy the inn to the fullest. It's all yours tonight."

"It's too big," she said. "Now I'm lonely."

I laughed again. "One day we'll get it just right, Goldilocks."

"Brunettes have more fun, darling. But I promise I will patch things up with our fair-haired family."

"Thanks for calling, Mom. It was good hearing your voice."

If she said goodbye I missed it because Percy was growling on my shoulder. He had been for some time but now it was louder. Since Keats was relaxed, I put two and two together.

"Louisa May?" I said. "Are you spying on me again?"

She emerged from the shadows of the house with Fanny on her shoulder. It was like looking into a mirror, only without a sheepdog. "It's not spying when someone's in your own backyard. Besides, Jilly kicked me out of the kitchen."

"That doesn't mean you can eavesdrop on private conversations."

"It's not private if you've got the phone on speaker. Your mom really projects. The whole neighborhood heard that conversation."

"Okay, you win. My mom means well, although it took me till this year to realize that." I watched as Lou sank onto the picnic bench and slumped a little. The day had taken a toll on her. "Your aunt means well, too, you know. She's worried about you."

"Worried about me? Why?"

"Because you've given up your life to come and watch over her. That's not what she wanted for you."

"She's been good to me. Paid most of my college tuition. I have a degree in business and communications that's pretty much useless here in Thistledown."

"Who says? We live in a digital economy now. I can think of a dozen things you could do, with just a bit of entrepreneurial spirit."

"I'm not your mother, Ivy. I can't start three businesses in a year."

"Be glad you're not my mother. She faced a ton of adversity raising six kids on her own and only hit her stride in her fifties."

She gave an impatient shrug that nearly dislodged Fanny. "I don't want to be your next project."

"You should be so lucky. I've rehabbed plenty of animals and apparently, one mother. Anyway, you heard the pep talk. There's a work of art inside you just waiting to get out. When I started chipping away at myself, I found a farmer-sleuth under the HR façade. What's your crusty attitude hiding?"

"Crusty! That's rude."

I shrugged, too, and Percy dug in for the ride. "Did it ever occur to you that your mood rubs off on your cat?"

She sat in silence for a few moments and then said, "Actually, I wouldn't mind some advice about Fanny. I love her to bits but after meeting Percy, I see she's a little intense."

"Living too small a life, maybe?"

"Maybe. I guess I sheltered her because of what happened to Yeats and Anne."

I sat down across from her. "It's a tough balance. My pets take a lot of risks and that scares me. But I do want them to live as big a life as they want."

Reaching up, she scratched Fanny's ears. "How do you know what's big enough?"

"They let me know. Fanny will let you know. Just give her a little more wiggle room."

She nodded and we both scooped our cats into our arms in the same moment.

"Your mom was wrong," she said. "My aunt doesn't want you to give Keats back."

"I know. My mom's just worried. She saw how my life changed after Keats."

"Got bigger?"

"Much bigger. Maybe that did rub off on her. With family, you never know where you end and someone else begins."

We got up from the bench at the same time and she turned. "I don't want Aunt Maud worrying about me. So, I'll consult with you and Jilly. When this is all done."

"You got it," I said. "We probably would have forced it on you anyway."

"It goes down easier with an invitation."

"Never stopped anyone in my family," I said.

The cats didn't even hiss as Keats herded us back to the door together. I had a feeling we'd all end up as friends eventually.

As long as Frost came home, that is.

CHAPTER NINETEEN

Just before dinner was ready, I got into the truck with Keats and Percy. Edna and Gertie had left the bush on the other side of town and wanted a lift back.

"No luck on the search," I told Keats, although he probably already knew that. "I'm sorry."

His mumble delivered the same message to me as it had to his breeder earlier. The game wasn't over. He wasn't particularly thrilled at the prospect of meeting his sister but seemed resigned it was going to happen. For the sake of Maud, he'd make the best of it.

The phone rang shortly after we left the driveway and I put Kellan on speaker. It was good to hear his voice fill the truck. For a second I wondered if this was a new fiancé tradition of checking in just for the sake of connection but his somber tone quickly reminded me that he was dealing with trouble at his end, as well. It seemed like ages since we'd spoken when in fact it was only about eight hours.

"Have you found the missing dog?" he asked.

I took the first turn into town. "Nope. It's the strangest thing. Lots of people saw Frost yesterday. She was clearly on the run, but whether it was because she was being chased or driven by hormones is unclear. Someone took her from the sitter's, but it's possible she escaped the dognapper, too."

"Hormones? What do you mean?"

"Frost's clock has been ticking," I said. "Maud Gentry hasn't been able to find a desirable sire but the dog may have taken matters into her own paws."

Kellan laughed and it was a welcome sound. I didn't hear it often enough—could never hear it often enough. There was precious little time between cases for him to become light-hearted again.

"Dogs will be dogs, I suppose," he said. "Maybe the situation isn't as dire as it initially seemed."

"Wouldn't that be nice for a change? There are far worse things than a litter of crossbreeds. Still, the dog has been on the run and no one's telling the truth about it. Thistledown is full of liars, it seems. Starting with Darnese Bibb."

"Darnese Bibb?" He sounded more alert now. "You've met someone by that name?"

"The dog-sitter. Couldn't get her facts straight to save her life. First she said the day was utterly peaceful, and then her story unraveled bit by bit. The dog escaped her clutches several times, it seems, and then was stolen overnight. Only Darnese's daughter, Sunny, has a key but as there's no sign of a break-in, I think it's another tall tale."

"I'm sure you're right," Kellan said. "If the dog's valuable, even only to Maud, there's a chance a ransom request will arrive."

"That's my hope," I said. "If it happens, we can rustle cash together. My current theory is that Darnese Bibb's son stole him. Kale's been gone for years, but even his own mom admits he was a bad seed."

There was a silence at the other end. A long one. "You said the dog disappeared only last night?"

"That's right. Sunny showed me photos that proved the dog was safe at her mom's place at bedtime. By morning... gone. My guess is that Kale Bibb found his way in and stole the dog. Could you check and see if you can find any dirt on him?"

The silence continued and Keats turned to me with a significant stare.

"Kellan? Are you still there?"

"Here. Just thinking."

I laughed. "I can feel the gears turning. Does the name ring a bell?"

"More like a siren," he said. "There's plenty of dirt on Kale Bibb. A record of petty crime that stretches as far as Boston."

"Ah. I take it the good job his sister said he had was a lie?"

"Depends on your definition of good, I suppose. Kale Bibb probably spun a few tales but I'm not sure he was bright enough to keep all his plates in the air."

Now I paused. "*Was?* As in, past tense."

"Correct. Kale Bibb is one person you can scratch off your list of potential suspects in Frost's disappearance. He wasn't available last night to break into his mother's home. He stopped being available for petty crime a couple of days ago. Permanently."

Percy meowed and I said, "I guess that explains the hankie."

"Hankie?" Kellan asked. "What hankie?"

"Never mind. I take it Darnese has no clue that her son has ended up... " My voice drifted off as my brain started doing the math. "Where exactly did Kale end up?"

"I think you know without my saying so, and I really can't say so until I've officially disclosed the news to his next of kin."

"I'll save you the trouble of telling me. Your dirt on Kale is literal. He was in the fresh grave Edna and Keats dowsed out this morning on the back country trails."

"I can neither confirm nor deny, but what we found there makes it very unlikely Kale visited his mom so recently."

Stopping at one of the two intersections in town, I noticed the background noise on his end for the first time. It sounded windy. "Are you driving?" I asked.

"Yeah. I'm on my way down there to visit Mrs. Bibb. Are *you* driving?"

"Just picking up Edna and Gertie from a diner. They were out searching on foot while I interviewed people."

"Which you need to stop doing, Ivy. There's an investigation underway."

I sat at the light long after it turned green, but there was no one behind me to honk. "I can't stop my investigation, Kellan. This is about Keats' sister. You encouraged me to come down here."

"That was before I knew who was in that grave, obviously. What if those two things are linked?"

"I'm revising my theory. It sounds like Kale was out of commission before the dog was taken."

"Nonetheless, it's a coincidence. Wouldn't you agree?"

It was a coincidence all right. How on earth did the son of Frost's sitter end up *under* the earth near Clover Grove around the same time the dog disappeared?

"Kellan, I have to rescue Keats' sister. Even more so now. You know that."

"What I know is that you've stumbled into something potentially dangerous. I need you to step aside until we've done our due diligence."

"It could take weeks to dig up all the facts strewn between Boston, Clover Grove and Thistledown. I'm not leaving Frost in limbo all that time."

"Ivy, it goes without saying that if there's a man dead, there's a killer at large."

"More likely in or around Clover Grove," I said. "Whereas here there's a dog in desperate need of help. She's family."

"You can't go running around a strange town stirring up suspicions. Especially right now." The wind got louder and I knew his boot was getting heavy on the gas pedal. "People are chatty in these situations. By the time breakfast is served, the stories will be locked down and harder to crack."

At the next intersection, I cruised through an amber light. If there were any police officers around, chances were they had their minds on Kellan's news.

"How about I promise not to interview anyone else before breakfast?"

"How about you promise not to interview anyone at all until we give you the all clear?"

I shook my head, trusting he'd sense my sadness across the miles. Being at odds with him bothered me more than ever now that there were rings on my finger. "That's a promise I can't make. I'll never stop talking to people when there's an animal at risk."

"You said yourself she may have run off in search of a canine paramour. Just stick with searching on foot for now."

My head was still shaking and he probably felt that, too. "I wish I could but this place is full of bad vibes."

His sigh was very audible over the wind in his vehicle. "There's not much we can do with bad vibes."

"I beg to differ. Keats can do plenty with bad vibes, and I bet his sister can, too. Maud seems to think Frost is among the smartest of all the dogs she's bred. A distillation of every great quality in the border collie, plus a little extra. She tried to keep that under wraps, since Keats and his dam were both stolen at sheepdog competitions. Darnese or Sunny may have told Kale, and he probably told someone else. If they know how valuable she is, a ransom note may never come."

The Busy Bee Diner came into view and I pulled over to finish the conversation with Kellan before Edna and Gertie could see the truck and join me.

After pondering a moment, Kellan said, "Why single out these dogs? Even if they are the best in breed."

Keats gave a cheeky rumble that made Kellan laugh.

"You heard the dog," I said. "He's proven his worth countless times, and unfortunately all the coverage would make it obvious to the wrong person."

"But why go after his sister instead of the great dog himself?"

"For the same reason someone stole their dam: to create more of them. Besides, Keats would never work for a crook, and maybe the thief is smart enough to know that. They need to train from the beginning so that the pup doesn't know any better."

"There are easier ways to pull off crimes around here," Kellan said. "Weapons. Technology. Criminal networks. A sheepdog hardly seems worth this fuss." He didn't wait for a canine protest to add, "No offense, Keats."

"He's giving my phone the stink eye," I said. "Anyway, there may be no link at all, but I'm still left with an obligation to find Frost and I need to fulfill it to the best of my ability. I will try not to step on your toes, but that's the best I can offer."

The sound of the wind shut off on his end, which only made his sigh louder. "Fine. Can you at least promise to stay safe? I put a ring on your finger to remind you I want you alive. Two rings, actually, because I wanted to underscore my point in red."

I laughed. "So that's what the garnets are all about."

"I've grown rather fond of you. And your priceless dog."

I ran a hand over Percy. "The cat's worth a bomb, too. I can only hope no one ever realizes the true value of my pets."

He fell silent again and I waited for him to end the conversation. It was the least I could do when I wouldn't step aside as he'd asked.

"We need to get those rings properly sized," he said, at last. "I'm afraid you'll lose them in the bush."

Keats gave a pant-laugh. *Busted.*

"Sized? What do you mean?"

"Ivy, if you think I haven't noticed the rubber washer on your finger, you underestimate me. I didn't make it to chief by missing things like a chunky rubber band parked over the jewels I chose with such care."

"These rings are perfect! I just need to gain a few pounds. Mandy's pie will take care of that."

"I've never heard a woman complain that sweets go straight to her fingers," he said, teasing me now.

"I don't want to take the rings off. It's bad luck and might jinx us." I decided to come completely clean. "You could have second thoughts."

"Won't happen. But those garnets have sentimental value and deserve better than returning to hill country soil."

"Won't happen," I echoed. "Because Keats will always find them. He's better than metal detectors, dowsing rods, and even ground penetrating radar."

"Huh. I'm beginning to see why the region's deadbeats might want to get their mitts on his sister. Cheaper, portable detection of valuables."

"She's a master of scent work," I said. "So let me find that canine gem before—"

The next words got swallowed by my scream.

CHAPTER TWENTY

"We talked about that," Edna said, laughing as she climbed into the passenger seat. "Soldiers don't scream like a girl."

I glared at her. "Soldiers don't ambush their friends."

"Exactly. You were lurking outside the diner for no good reason. Gertie and I decided to beat you at your own game."

"I was only—"

"Oh, we know what you were doing," Edna said. "You had a moony look that said you were talking to Chief Fiancé about things unrelated to the current case."

Keats grumbled agreement. The conversation with Kellan had been a few beats too long for the dog, too.

"We're right, aren't we, Chief?" Gertie asked, from the back seat.

"Bye, ladies," he said, and disconnected quickly.

"Has to have the last word, doesn't he?" Edna said. "A word he knows we dislike almost as much as 'old.'"

"Kellan and I talked about the current cases," I said, pulling an illegal U-turn on the main drag. "Plural. If you'd care to apologize, I might fill you in on the other one."

Edna pulled off her helmet and patted her curls. "Do we really need to know? Apologies are hard to come by in my world."

"I'm sorry, Ivy," Gertie said. "I shouldn't have let Edna talk me into it."

Turning in her seat, Edna scowled. "Nice try. This one was your idea and I'm not going to squander an apology when Ivy had no business wasting our time. We've been wearing out boot leather for hours looking for her canine niece."

"Niece? Well, I guess that's as good a term as any," I said, pushing the pedal down. "We can forfeit the apology just this once."

"Can we forfeit the velocity?" Gertie said. "Normally I enjoy a thrill ride but the onion rings I ate at the Busy Bee are arguing with my gall bladder."

"You still have yours?" Edna asked, patting her abdomen. "That was the first thing to go for me. Left more room for my lungs to expand."

I waited for them to simmer down then shared Kellan's news about the grave they'd happened upon that morning. The excitement level in the truck soared. They high-fived each other with gloved hands.

"See, Ivy?" Edna said. "We struck gold and you doubted."

Gertie leaned between the seats. "I'd hardly call a Thistledown deadbeat gold, old friend. We can do better."

"Just a beginning," Edna said. "I wish I didn't have to hang up my dowsing rod for winter. The chief is going to want us on retainer."

I let them bask in their success because they deserved a moment of glory. These two were always on the move, learning new skills and defying all expectations for people of their generation—especially women. On top of that, they had spent the day combing the bush for my dog's sister and would continue in the morning without a complaint.

Well, there would be complaints but mostly for dramatic effect.

"How does the discovery of the Bibb body connect with the missing dog?" Gertie asked, as I pulled into the Gentry driveway.

"We've got all night to speculate," I said. "Maud insisted we stay here and given what's happened, it seems like a good idea. Lou's setting up cots in the living room, like a proper barracks."

"What fun." Edna's voice was full of genuine enthusiasm. "We can tell ghost stories later. Separate the women from the girls."

I laughed. "You can have the win, given your accomplishment today."

They were already hopping out of the truck and both turned to stare at me when I didn't turn off the truck or make a move to join them. "Where do you think you're going?" Edna said. "I highly doubt the chief would endorse a solo mission in these circumstances."

"I promised to pick up groceries for breakfast," I said. "Won't be long."

The truck started rolling and there was a 50:50 chance they'd hop back in. I hoped their desire to go inside and spill the story of Kale Bibb would tip the balance.

One slam. Two slams.

Keats gave a ha-ha-ha as I turned on a dime and beat it back into town.

I ignored another amber light on Main Street. Luckily, I knew the cops had bigger fish to fry than my rolling stops. They'd refused to devote any manpower to a missing dog case but would have little choice about following up on a homeboy gone wrong. If I had my way, I would use their distraction to my advantage.

With his paws on the dash, Keats urged me on. As we parked in front of the diner, the man and woman I'd seen earlier emerged from the alley. They turned right to walk out of town.

Letting the boys out, I followed, careful not to startle the couple.

"Excuse me," I said. "Rickie? Madge?"

They turned with a mixture of annoyance and unease in their eyes. I had guessed correctly, but it hadn't been a huge leap. Both were overdressed for the weather in puffy down coats that had seen better days, hats, scarves, snow pants, heavy gloves and boots. The true giveaways were permanently ruddy cheeks and chapped lips. Year-round exposure to the elements had taken a toll.

"Who wants to know?" Rickie Merriweather asked.

I stuck out my hand and he batted it away, just as they'd batted away an entire community where they apparently felt spurned and even scorned. If I'd arrived a little sooner, I would have offered to buy them dinner at the Busy Bee Diner, so that they didn't need to visit the dumpster beside it. But I sensed meeting Edna and Gertie would have been too much for them. It was too much for most people.

"I'm Ivy Galloway, and these are my boys. The cat is Percy, and the dog, Keats." I gestured to my pets and the movement sent Madge reeling backward a couple of steps. She probably lived in a chronic state of stress. "I wanted to ask a few questions."

"You only get one," Rickie said. "And we don't commit to answering."

"I'm in town from Clover Grove to visit Maud Gentry," I said. "My dog once belonged to her before he was stolen at a—"

"Am I missing the question?" Rickie interrupted. "We don't have all night."

"Sorry," I said. "I wanted to set the context and—"

"We're off the grid, not off our rockers," Madge said. Her voice sounded rough, as if she'd been swallowing icicles. "We heard the gossip. Some people still talk to us."

"Then you know we're here to help find Frost. My dog's sister."

"We know your crazy friends were stomping around in our backyard all day."

"Your yard?"

Rickie made a sweeping gesture. "We live off this land. It's all our yard now."

"We followed your friends here to study them," his wife said. "They're obviously doing something right. Never seemed to mind the wind or the cold."

"It's all about the right gear, or so they tell me," I said. "They're preparing for... well, tough times."

"Good," Madge said. "We know tough times and wish we'd prepared better. Didn't see it coming, I'm afraid."

Rickie's wary eyes turned haunted. "I'm sorry, hon. I made some bad choices."

She reached for his glove. "And one good one. We're in this together."

I wanted to fade away then, leave this couple in whatever peace they found in a harsh life, but Keats poked me in the shin. Now wasn't the time for delicacy, it seemed. Rickie turned back after a moment and there was a flicker of light in his eyes. It came from the flashing diner sign but possibly also from the love his wife still had for him.

"Do you have any idea where Frost is?" I asked. "It sounds like Maud was right when she said you know this land inside and out."

"Why would we tell you?" he said. "Sounds like you bring nothing but trouble on your animals."

The words struck like a snowmobile boot to the gut because they had the ring of truth. Keats mumbled something defiant in my defense, however, and Percy scaled my back to stare at the couple from my shoulder.

"They like her, Rickie," Madge said. "No matter what some say." She blew out a frosty gust. "Not that we care much what people say."

Keats mumbled again and his tone was kinder. It sounded like a question. I didn't understand it but perhaps Rickie did, because he said, "We had to give up our dog. The life we chose wasn't fair to pets. My biggest regret."

"Maud helped with that," Madge said. "Found a good home for the dog on a farm. He's happy now."

I clasped my hands, feeling the rubber ring under the left glove. Kellan would probably consider this meddling. It *was* meddling.

"Maud wants to help more but says you prefer to go your own way. All I want to know is whether you've seen Frost."

Rickie shook his head but Keats told me otherwise. And then he told the man otherwise, since they seemed to have established a level of understanding.

"Frost ran away from Darnese Bibb for a reason," Madge said. "The dog knows her way home and I expect she'll head back when she feels safe."

"But that's the thing," I said. "She's not safe. Someone stole her from Darnese's house."

They glanced at each other and silently agreed to cut me a little slack. "She got away," Madge said. "Left a trail of blood in the first sprinkle of snow last night."

I gasped. "Where? I need to find her and get her to a vet."

"Not Frost's blood," Madge said, skirting my question. "Her

kidnapper's. At least, so we assumed. There was a bit of navy blue fabric hooked over her tooth and footprints that melted this morning."

"Then what happened?" My voice spiked a little. "And where is she now?"

"Safe," Rickie said. "We made sure of that. Would have told Maud directly but when we got there, you folks were unloading. Can't handle crowds anymore. Especially not people in camo and ponchos."

"With rifles," his wife added.

Keats left my side and circled the pair. "Can we go and get Frost, please? My dog wants to meet his sister."

They exchanged another look and I felt the "no" before it came out.

"We'll bring her back when it's safe," Madge said. "You've said yourself it's not."

They started to shuffle backward and I followed. "I hope it doesn't sound like bragging, but we're the closest thing this dog can get to safety right now. Keats will fight to the death for Frost."

He mumbled something noncommittal. A let's-meet-her-first kind of comment, but I knew he would do just that.

Still, the Merriweathers refused, backing ahead of me faster and faster. They faded into the darkness of a side street.

"You leave me no choice," I called after them. "Keats?"

There was a man squeal as Rickie felt the sheepdog pinch through his snow pants. "Hey," he said. "Your sister doesn't bite."

Keats gave a pant-laugh, happy to be ahead in this regard.

"Let's find out," I said, catching up to them.

"We're not taking you to our home," Madge said. "We have so little left, you see."

My stomach twisted into a knot of shame over forcing the

issue. "I know, and I'm sorry to violate your privacy. But I've made a commitment to Maud and whether you lead me there or not, we will find her. The sooner we go, the sooner you're rid of us."

Rickie looked from me to his wife. "Guess she can't be all bad."

"Not even half bad," I said. "And I promise you I will forget I ever saw your place."

CHAPTER TWENTY-ONE

I needed to stop making promises I couldn't keep. It was nearly impossible to forget anything I wanted to forget. My brain was extremely capricious after the concussion and marched to its own drummer.

As I marched through the bush with Madge and Rickie Merriweather, however, I realized I didn't even want to forget this moment, or this place. It was a beautiful albeit cold evening with a full moon hanging overhead like a simple, classy Christmas tree ornament.

The couple moved with ease through a thread of a trail uphill and down for nearly a mile, or so it felt. Perhaps I should have been nervous, but with Keats in the lead and Percy on my shoulder, I was reasonably confident they meant me no harm. In fact, Madge kept up a dialogue with Keats that eluded me, and, it turned out, her husband as well.

Turning at one point, he said, "They seem to understand each other. She was always good with dogs."

"I've rarely seen him take to anyone so quickly. Your wife is a special lady, Rickie."

His eyes were pools of darkness but I felt them scanning me.

"I suppose you are, too," he said. "Otherwise, that dog wouldn't throw down for you. We've read stories in the newspaper. Thelma Tilrow always lets us have a copy at library closing. Helps pass an evening."

"Thelma is a friend of our librarian in Clover Grove. Does she know you have Frost?"

His toque rustled against the nylon coat as he shook his head. "Didn't say a word to anyone. The dog came to us and we couldn't turn her away."

"She knew where you lived?"

"Visited now and then when she was out with Maud. We had an agreement."

"I believe you," I said. "Based on our general direction, I think Frost may have been trying to get to you yesterday morning when she bolted out of Elmer Mogus's yard. Seems like she knew where to go for help."

"Our home is her home for as long as she wants it," he said. "Madge? Honey, what's wrong?"

His wife had stopped walking. Ahead of her, Keats puffed and went into a point.

"Rickie," she said, her rough voice now raw, "we've been robbed."

The large prefab shed that must have been their home had been vandalized. One side was bashed in and the window on the other was broken. The light of the moon revealed their possessions strewn over the hard earth of the small clearing.

It hurt my heart to see such humble lodgings violated. Only someone without a shred of human decency could stoop to such action.

"She's gone," Madge said. "Frost is gone."

Percy jumped down from my shoulder and began investigating the clearing with Keats. All fur flags settled and the next leg of our journey began.

"It's okay, Madge," I said. "The boys say there's still hope. I'm sure they can track her, but maybe you have an idea where she'd go from here."

The couple exchanged another silent communication and turned in unison. We trudged another half mile or so through the bush along a trail that looked nearly the same as the last one. I figured we'd emerge in front of a second shed that may be in worse shape than the first.

Instead, when the forest opened, the moon's light streamed over a beautiful log house that seemed in perfect condition. The front walk under our boots bore the marks of sweeping, although there was no sign of current habitation. It was dark, the curtains were closed, and there was no smoke coming from the chimney.

"Is this yours?" I asked.

"Oh, we wish," Madge said, with a light laugh. Glancing quickly at her husband, she added, "Not really, though. Too much house for us. We're happy staying in the little guest cabin behind now and then."

"We're not squatting, if that's what you're thinking," Rickie said. "The owner invited us to stay there as long as we keep an eye on the place. He's only up this way a few weeks a year."

"Sounds like a great arrangement to me," I said. "He'd need a property manager."

"In fact, the deal was that we could stay in the big house, as long as we left it like we found it," Rickie said. "But it didn't feel right to us and eventually it would have raised questions. This-tledown is like that. They feel guilty about us but wouldn't want to see us basking in luxury, either."

I wanted to protest, but suspected it was true enough. Clover Grove had a similar mentality. "Then you found a good compromise. But why stay in the shed you showed me? It didn't seem fit for a hill country winter."

Rickie laughed. "It's not winter, yet. Barely Thanksgiving. We don't want to get spoiled by the good life, so we only move here when the going gets really tough."

I didn't know what to say about that. By my standards, the going was tougher than I could bear already.

Madge touched my sleeve. "Don't pity us or feel bad about what you have, Ivy. We chose this life. It feels good to us to be in alignment with our values."

"I get that," I said. "It's important for me to be in alignment with my values, too."

"You ladies want to stand around having a heart-to-heart? Or do you want to find this dog? Because unless I'm much mistaken, the mumbler here thinks a family reunion is in order."

My eyes darted to Keats and saw he was trembling under his jacket. It wasn't cold enough for that, and normally I only saw him quake in the presence of a body of water, great or small.

"Lead on, buddy," I said, and the rest of us shuffled forward to circle the log house.

About 15 yards behind the main structure stood a small, adorable cabin. With a dusting of snow, it would resemble a Christmas gingerbread house, minus the candy.

Rickie gave me a nudge to keep going. "The woodshed behind is the perfect place for—"

A tornado of fur shot around the gingerbread house. I might have expected Frost to run to Rickie and Madge, or even her canine brother. Instead, she raced toward me, leapt and hit me square in the chest, sending Percy flying with a yowl of disgust.

My arms came up and pinwheeled. I was afraid of striking her as she leapt again and decided collapsing was the better course of action.

It was a wonderful moment—one of the best and brightest in a life of many great moments—to see the brown sheepdog standing on my ribcage and staring down at me. Her green eyes had a spooky glow that might have made me nervous if she hadn't given my cheek a sloppy lick. She followed that with a mumble that was similar to Keats', though noticeably higher. Frost sounded like a younger, more feminine version of my own beloved dog.

"Hey, girl," I said. "Nice to meet you."

In truth, I felt like I already knew her. If she let me up, I suspected I would be able to understand a good bit of what she was telling me and quickly learn the rest. Most new animals I met came with a unique and complicated language but in this case, it was more like a change in dialect.

A louder and deeper mumble came out of the darkness beside me, followed by the clacking of canine teeth as Keats offered his sister an air snap.

"Stop that," I told him. "She's been through a lot. Let her have a second."

Frost was no pushover, however. She grumbled right back at Keats and another set of canine teeth clattered as she matched him snap for snap.

"They won't fight, will they?" Madge asked. "I would hate for Maud to get her dog back even more banged up."

I gently pushed Frost off my chest, sat up and pulled out my phone to shine the light on her. Along with the surgical dressing on her front paw, she was wearing a cute blue jacket dotted with white poodles. It had a faux fur ruff, and as I admired it, she pranced sideways and back. Someone didn't mind her coat at all.

"The jacket belonged to our dog," Madge said. "Today I was glad I'd held onto it. We tried not to get too sentimental about material things when we made our move."

I pushed myself off the cold earth. "You've both been very kind to her. I hope you agree to let her come home now."

Their heads bobbed in unison. "Only because of you,"

Madge said. "The dog seems to trust you. And yet it sounds like you've never met before."

I texted both Maud and Edna to tell them the news, while Keats and Frost circled each other. To an outsider, it may well have looked like a fight waiting to happen but I knew from their stance that each was treating the other like a... well, a sheep, to be precise. Their fixed gazes and mirrored crouches were about out-herding each other. It was a joint language carefully encoded in their genes by a diligent breeder.

"We've never met before," I confirmed, taking a photo and sending it to Maud, Lou and Jilly. "But it seems like we're family. To be honest, that happens with a lot of my animals. It's usually not instantaneous, but we get there."

"We know you'll protect her," Rickie said. "It's not that we don't think Maud and Louisa would try to do the same, but I think even the dog knows they can't. Someone is after her."

Frost stopped the herding game and stared around the circle with her eerie eyes. A shiver ran through us all at once.

"Let's get moving," I said, scooping up Percy to keep him out of the dogs' way. "I promise you I will put everything I've got into keeping this dog safe." Keats ambushed his sister, nearly knocking her down. It was a cheat move because she was focused on us. I shook my glove at him and said, "Play nice. She has an injured paw. There will be plenty of time for hijinks once we figure out the rest of the puzzle."

"You mean figure out who's trying to steal her?" Rickie asked. "Because we know the answer to that. It's Kale Bibb. We saw him in Thistledown a couple of times this month. He met up with his sister, Sunny, and I guess that's how he heard Frost would be staying with Darnese. Saw his chance and jumped on it."

"He was like that even in school," his wife continued. "Always looking for a quick buck even if it wasn't a clean buck."

I was glad they couldn't see my face. Since the two dogs were vying for the lead it made sense for me to walk ahead and monitor them. They were behaving as if they'd known each other all their lives. Keats had never shown such interest in any dog before, even Clem. Mind you, there was no deference or respect between them. It was a sibling vibe, similar to what I shared with Asher. Despite being an officer of the law and a married man, my brother enjoyed creeping up to startle me and even roughhousing on occasion. My scream was his reward. Far from resenting it, I actually enjoyed the camaraderie. Life was plenty serious enough without entirely cutting off play.

"I believe the police are exploring any connection to Kale Bibb," I told the Merriweathers. "Did he come home alone or with friends?"

"I only saw him with Sunny," Madge said. "How about you, hon?"

Rickie waited a few beats and then said, "Saw Kale lurking by the pond a couple of times and assumed he was waiting for his sister. But one day he left with someone else in a hooded jacket. Taller than Kale, so I'd say it was another man."

"Don't worry," I said. "The key thing now is just to make sure Frost has round-the-clock supervision until the police get to the bottom of it."

Someone behind me blew a raspberry. "The police are never around when they're needed," Madge said. "We've been bullied dozens of times by local kids—and a few adults—and no cop has ever intervened on our behalf."

I glanced over my shoulder. "This time it's different. Our police from Clover Grove are on their way down right now. The chief is my—well, my fiancé."

It felt awkward using the word in these circumstances. "Fiancé" seemed like a term for happier times.

"Don't feel embarrassed about finding your love match," Madge said. "I'm still a romantic after decades with my man."

I turned away quickly to avoid seeing the kiss land, although the noise stopped the dogs in their tracks.

Now we were close enough to the Busy Bee Diner that neon lights flashed off the trees, and by the time we stepped into the parking lot near the dumpster, Maud Gentry was on her knees with arms outstretched, backed by Edna, Gertie, Jilly and Louisa.

Frost left her brother without a backward glance and raced to her owner. This time, she pulled up short to avoid knocking Maud down, spinning instead in a frenzy of joy.

There were tears all around including a loud, honking snort from Rickie. Only Edna kept a stiff upper lip, continuing to scan for threats.

"Let's all go inside and wait for Kellan," Jilly said, taking Percy from my arms and hugging him. "This is cause for celebration."

I looked at Keats and he looked at Frost. Six eerie eyes turned back to me. Even Keats' brown eye cast a neon glow, reflecting the diner's sign.

It wasn't time to celebrate yet.

Not by a long shot.

CHAPTER TWENTY-TWO

The next morning was a little challenging, despite the happy resolution to our mission. After a restless night on a cot in the Gentry living room, I couldn't escape to burn off energy in any of my usual ways. Kellan and his colleague from the regional police had ordered us to stay put and the small house was overstuffed with people and pets who didn't like to be inside at the best of times. We were getting on each other's nerves simply by breathing.

That said, we all covered it up well, with plenty of conversation to get to know each other. With her dog home, Maud warmed considerably and did her best to make everyone comfortable. Jilly ordered a delivery of groceries from Fresh Pickens and started cooking up a storm. It was funny that she had to come so far to get some alone time in a small kitchen that wasn't her own.

Meanwhile, I had never missed my manure pile more. Keats trailed after me from room to room, grumbling. He wanted to be doing. At that point, he may even have lowered himself to play fetch.

"Always knew that dog would have trouble settling," Maud

said, as we stood by the front door watching the police come and go at Darnese Bibb's house up the street. "He was restless even as a young pup. From the time his eyes opened, he started looking for you."

I turned to her in surprise. "For me?"

"That's what I assume now, anyway. Some dogs crave a human connection from the get-go and that was Yeats." She gave me a sly grin. "I've decided to keep calling him that because it was his name when our story began. His mother was the same, and I was the instant target of Anne's attachment. Yeats was different. He listened even better than his dam, but he always seemed to be looking past me or through me."

"It's the blue eye," I said. "Seems like it looks into another dimension."

She flapped dismissive fingers. "I don't believe in such things. And remember, his mom had two eyes like that. I know that dog was looking for a different leader. Apparently, it was you. His eyes, blue and brown, rarely leave you."

My fingers dropped to his head and the dog and I exchanged a sloppy smile of utter devotion.

"I'm glad you're okay with... well, everything," I told her.

"Before I agree to that, could you be more specific?"

I used my thumbnail to scratch at a bloom of frost on the glass. "As you said earlier, we seem to end up in complicated situations more than you would probably like for one of your dogs."

She stared up the road for a moment before answering. "Would I like every one of my dogs to be pampered parlor pets? Not really. I bred them for great things and Yeats is living out his potential as Keats. I'm proud of what he became. There are fewer criminals around because of the work you do together. You make the world a better place."

My eyelids fluttered, determined to hold back the tears. "What about Frost? What's her destiny?"

Maud's fingers dropped to the brown ears. "Puppies, I hope. More brilliant dogs to do great things. I confess I'd prefer to keep her off the frontlines of crime-fighting. I am not you."

In a rash moment, I caught her hand, knowing we were both allergic to PDAs. "You've given me such a gift. There is nothing I wouldn't do for Keats." The dog grumbled a protest and I added, "Other than let him run around without a coat in winter."

That broke the tension and she pulled her fingers out of my grasp. "Honestly, Yeats. Man up and wear your coat without whining. Your sister has quite a collection and loves them."

He mumbled an insolent response and I shook my head. "No need for a coat today, since we're practically prisoners."

"My roof isn't going to contain your friends for long," she said. "Edna was talking about doing group calisthenics and Gertie agreed. I can only hope to have half that energy at their age."

I laughed. "I've got another plan if you'll cover for me. That's my brother coming toward us to check on Jilly. I'll ask her to keep him here so that you're all safe, and slip out the side door with Keats. There's someone I want to visit."

She didn't give me a nod straight away. "May I ask whom?"

"It's better if you don't. Easier to give a straight answer to the law."

Looking down at Keats, she said, "Do I have any choice, sir?"

He gave a pant-laugh, white paws pounding the doormat. It was a hard no.

I caught Frost's eye and said, "Take care of everyone here, will you? We'll be back soon."

She echoed her brother's pant-laugh, and I decided to take it as a yes, although it wasn't. Frost would likely do what she considered the right thing by her own moral code. I just didn't know the parameters yet.

"I've never heard her do that before," Maud said as I grabbed my coat out of the pile on a chair and picked up Keats' coat from the floor. "Did she just learn to laugh from her brother?"

"Could be worse," I said, slipping into the kitchen, where Jilly was making quite a mess. "And it probably will be."

Maud stepped into the living room and announced loudly, "Ready for some jumping jacks, Edna. Bring on your soldier moves."

KEATS LED PERCY and me through the back hedge, and into the bush on a circuitous route that dropped me exactly where I wanted to be: the Thistledown Public Library.

I was in the right place, but regrettably someone had arrived ahead of me.

A beat-up sedan I knew well was blocking the ramp to the front door.

"Oh no," I said. "Did she actually follow the police down here? Kellan is going to be furious. And poor Thelma. She has no idea what she's— Okay. Wow."

Thelma Tilrow backed Justine Schalow right out the front door and halfway down the ramp. She was holding an old-fashioned wooden pointer and jabbing it like a rapier in Justine's general direction. The weapon suited the schoolhouse perfectly.

"Go," Thelma said. "I will not be browbeaten by a reporter in my own library. Or anywhere for that matter."

"Madam, this is your opportunity to do the right thing for your town," Justine said. "To be a local hero."

Thelma jabbed again and Justine jumped back a few steps, arms flailing as she tried to find her balance on the ramp. She could have grabbed the railing but probably didn't want to show weakness.

"I don't need instructions on how to contribute to my community," Thelma said. "Especially not from a reporter with a rather dubious track record. Find your own story."

"That's what I was trying to do when you cut me off."

The pointer swept in a wide arc. "Do not come into my house and make a mess of my things. It's disrespectful. You'll need to find another way to break the news."

"It's a public library, not your house," Justine said. "I'll come back with the police and you'll have to let me in."

"Go right ahead." Thelma poked and prodded till Justine continued her retreat. "I'll be happy to give Chief Jerry Garveth a piece of my mind. It won't be the first."

"Can you really spare those pieces?" Justine asked. "At this stage of life, you—"

The last word came out as a squawk when pointer connected with ribcage. Justine backed down the ramp and opened her car door.

"I can still run circles around a smart-aleck reporter," Thelma said, following her.

Justine got into the car and said something that earned her car a swat with the poker. Another dent wasn't going to make a difference.

Hauling back for a good swing, Thelma fired off a few words I didn't expect to hear from a librarian. It made me wonder what Dottie was capable of doing when riled. Regardless, I wanted Thelma on my team at the end times. I'd choose the librarians first.

She brandished the pointer long enough to send Justine off in a cloud of dust before turning to walk up the ramp.

"You can come out of the bushes now, scaredy pants," she called in my direction. "And if you and your pets show enough respect, I might tell you what I wouldn't tell your nemesis."

CHAPTER TWENTY-THREE

This time Thelma actually welcomed us into the library and I was surprised to have Justine Schalow to thank for that.

Not that I would ever give her that satisfaction, but I acknowledged my gratitude with an inner smile. Justine was the worst kind of thorn in my side but she made me a better sleuth. I couldn't rest on my laurels when the reporter was either one step behind me, or in this case, possibly a step ahead. The only saving grace was that Justine annoyed everyone else as much as she did me. As long as I could annoy people less, I would be okay. My HR training still had me covered in that regard.

The layout inside was the same as Dottie's in Clover Grove. Maybe that was something they'd learned in library school, along with the repertoire of disapproving facial expressions. The front desk, the book stacks and computers were almost identically arranged. I could find the romantic poets in seconds if I had time for a trip down memory lane.

Thelma's eyes narrowed over her half-moon glasses to tell me I didn't. Justine must have been moving in the right direction to find out who killed Kale Bibb. Technically, we were all working on the same team to bring someone to justice, I supposed, but our motivation was different. Justine wanted a story, whereas I wanted Maud, Louisa, Frost and the entire community to be safe. I wasn't sure how—or even if—the two threads of the mystery crossed but Keats' prickly posture indicated we needed to proceed under that assumption, and Percy's twitching tail as he made himself at home on Thelma's stool told me to get a move on it.

"Please remove the cat," she said. "That's my—"

"Throne?" I interrupted.

"Cockpit might be more appropriate. Regardless, I don't want orange fur on my skirt. I chose to wear my best black suit today out of respect to the surviving Bibbs. I see you chose to wear bibbed overalls."

I smoothed my usual uniform. "They're clean, though. My other pair got a little banged up when Frost tackled me last night." Her eyes widened and I quickly added, "She was glad to see me."

"She doesn't know you," Thelma said. "Why would she greet you so warmly?"

"We all know each other," I said, running my finger along a row of books on a cart and wishing I had time to organize them properly. "The good guys, I mean. The animal lovers." I pulled out a heavy book that turned out to be an encyclopedia of dogs. "You're one of them, Thelma. As is Dottie Bridges."

She tried to shoo Percy by flapping a file folder and succeeded only in relocating him onto her desk. "Don't lump me in with your motley crew. I'm just trying to keep my little corner of hill country safe."

"A laudable goal." I put the book back, as tempting as it was to flip through it. "What did Justine want?"

"The same thing every reporter wants: to be first to expose the story of how the hometown boy went wrong. She grilled me on Kale Bibb's childhood in hopes of figuring out how he ended up under the earth in Clover Grove."

"Were you able to enlighten her?"

"Able but unwilling," Thelma said. "It was a sad story, but I know you have a sad story, too, so I don't mind telling you that Kale's father, Oscar Bibb, was part of the last generation of hill country ruffians and con artists. He was a handsome man and Darnese didn't have the sense or confidence to keep her distance. By all accounts, he was abusive and the only good thing he ever did was get himself run off a cliff before his children reached high school. Kale was a nice boy when he came out for my enrichment programs. Later, he lost his way."

"Kale had a record, I heard."

She handed the file folder to me. "Petty crime. Honestly, I don't think Kale had the wherewithal to spearhead anything serious. He was more of a follower, and that's what got him into bigger trouble. There's always a smart sociopath looking to lead a lost kid like Kale astray."

"Sadly, that appears to be a hill country tradition," I said. "My father ran into similar problems."

"Dottie said Calvin had a little more going for him upstairs." Thelma tapped her stiff curls, which looked exactly as they had the day before. "Sunny does, too, and with her brother gone, perhaps things will turn out better for her."

"The Merriweathers told me Sunny and Kale met up a few times recently."

Thelma nodded. "Rickie and Madge are my eyes and ears in the community. Both good souls. That's the only reason I'm entertaining you today. They said you were kind to them."

"Of course I was kind to them. They're a nice couple and I respect they're living life on their own terms, even if it seems like a difficult path to me."

"Very much so. I do what I can to help but they won't accept much, unfortunately."

"There's a reward for finding Frost. I hope they'll take it."

Her frown said otherwise. "They said Frost found them, and they refused to surrender her until you arrived. So they won't take the money, although no one around here needs it more."

I opened the folder and scanned the clippings about Kale. They were short reports of minor crimes, starting with vandalism, trespassing, drug possession and breaking and entering. His criminal trajectory seemed to stall for a few years and then picked up again in Boston. The crimes got a little bigger, and he'd been detained recently.

"Who paid his bail, I wonder?" I tapped that article. "Darnese didn't seem to know he was around."

"And you believe her?" Thelma asked.

"Keats and Percy believed her. They're my traveling lie detectors. But Sunny was evasive."

Thelma pursed her lips and made circles with her index finger to hurry my review. "Your pushy friend strikes me as the type who doesn't give up easily. She'll be back before long."

"Justine Schalow is not my friend. Notice I didn't dispute the word nemesis."

"Notice the clock ticking." Her index finger spun faster. "I bet Justine doesn't expect to be spoon-fed."

Her jibes had the desired effect of making me focus on the file. The last three items were photographs. One was of Sunny and a young man with similar pointy features and small eyes, no doubt inherited from Darnese.

The next photo was of two men—Kale and someone else, wearing a rust-colored baseball cap and a navy blue windbreaker. I had seen that cap and windbreaker before on Sunny's phone. She'd been hiking in the hills with this guy.

"Interesting," I said. "You seem to have a side hustle as a spy, Thelma."

She snorted. "Hardly. I'm not the type of person who escapes attention down by the pond."

I gave her a little grin. "I suppose the curls might give you away."

Patting the stiff helmet of gray sausages, she puckered again. "You young people underestimate the utility of a good set. I curl once and don't need to think about my hair for days."

My index finger copied her earlier motion. "If you didn't take these photos, who did?"

"Rickie Merriweather. I got him a cheap phone so that I could make sure they were okay. He has gout and I pick up his medication."

"He returns the favor with intel," I said. "Going where curls cannot."

"I consider any help I give them being neighborly," she said, primly. "But they hate handouts, so they found a way to show their appreciation. Information is definitely currency in my books."

"Mine too. Do you know the man in the navy windbreaker? His face is always turned away from the camera."

Thelma's smugness faded. "I hoped you would."

Keats' blue eye was on me and he offered a noncommittal mumble. "Maybe I do, but information often isn't filed properly in my mental archives. There's a bad elf in there who doesn't know the Dewey decimal system. Can you give me a clue?"

"Another clue? It sounds like Dottie misled me about your initiative."

I pulled out my phone and snapped photos of everything in the file. "The police might find him first."

The half-moon glasses slipped down her nose and she tossed in an eye roll for good measure. "Our regional police are bumbling fools. They'll throw every possible obstacle into your fiancé's path, accidentally or on purpose. I'm sure the fellow in the windbreaker is behind Kale's death and I count on you to get the job done before he strikes again."

"I'll track Rickie down and see if he knows more," I said, heading for the door. "The Merriweathers are probably trying to put their home back together."

I was nearly at the bottom of the ramp when Thelma cleared her throat behind me. "You could have a word with Wendel Barrick, first. When he came to collect the books he ordered, he mentioned someone had shown too much interest in his dog. I believe it's a border collie."

Turning, I glared at her. "You didn't think to mention this earlier?"

"I thought about it and decided against it. As I said, I'm not in the business of spoon-feeding capable young women. Imagine how much more satisfying the conclusion will be if you put your own pieces together."

"Imagine how much safer Frost and everyone else will be if we resolve this sooner." Keats mumbled something and I added, "It's like you withheld a key piece of the jigsaw puzzle."

The shoulders of her black blazer rose and fell. "Dottie bragged about you as if you were her own personal savant. I was eager to put you to the test. Sadly, you're not impressing me so far."

I flicked my finger at Percy, who'd come out last. He lashed his tail, took an almost perpendicular leap, and smacked Thelma between her shoulder blades.

The gasp and scream that followed were decidedly not in the librarian handbook.

"You failed my test, too, Miss Tilrow. But mark my words, I'll fit the last piece of the puzzle into place today and you can add another clipping to my file."

Percy jumped to the railing and swaggered toward me, while Thelma tried to sweep fur off her back. Her gyrations made me smile.

"I suppose you'll want an address for Wendel? Perhaps a handy list of the books he has on loan?"

"We'll manage just fine without your assistance, thank you."

"One thing is sure," she called after me. "You're every bit as cocky as Dottie says."

Keats' mumble was worse than cocky and she stopped sweeping her back to shake a finger at him.

"Sorry," I said, heading back into the bush. "Not sorry."

CHAPTER TWENTY-FOUR

K eats and Percy had no trouble locating Wendel Barrick's house, probably just from the scent of the man's sheepdog. I kept to the bush till we arrived in his yard and ignored the pinging of my phone. The only reason someone hadn't already come after me was that Asher was guarding Maud's house. No one could get in or out. That meant I was on my own, but for the moment, I preferred it that way.

Not that I was ever alone when I had my boys with me.

It was mid-afternoon when I knocked at Mr. Barrick's side door. I couldn't risk being seen on the front porch in case Kellan got wind of it from the neighbors.

A gentleman of about Thelma's vintage cracked open the door. A beam of light bounced off his balding head and gold wire-rimmed glasses. But it was a movement from below that caught my eye. A black muzzle poked through the crack and drew in a long, audible snort.

Keats mumbled something to the dog that sounded oddly polite for him. I could only assume the dog was elderly, as few fellow canines won such respect at first sniff.

"Hello, Mr. Barrick," I said. "Thelma Tilrow sent me over. I wanted to meet your dog."

"George isn't receiving guests today. Nor am I. Do you know there's been a murder, young lady?"

"I do, sir. My fiancé is the chief of police from Clover Grove. He came down to help with the investigation."

"Then perhaps you should leave the work to the men," he said. "That's no business for a woman."

My inner hackles rose, but my first-class HR smile also rose. "There's a woman on Chief Harper's team, actually. He'd like to recruit more but so few throw their bonnets into the ring."

"I see. You're one of those feminists. My granddaughter is the same and it's only going to make her miserable in life."

"I don't find labels like that very useful, sir. I'm a hobby farmer and an innkeeper. Those are labels I own. But most importantly, I'm an animal lover, and that's something we have in common, I'll bet. If you want handy labels, my name is Ivy. My dog is Keats and my cat, Percy."

The door cracked open a little more. "Fine-looking sheepdog, I'll grant you that. Is he a good farmhand?"

"Excellent. We have quite a range of rescue animals, from camelids to an emu, and he manages them all with ease. How about your dog?"

"We had a farm just outside of Thistledown and I couldn't have run it without George. I retired him when my wife wanted to move into the town proper. Then she passed, and I'm stuck here."

I noticed the silver fur on the dog's muzzle and realized he was probably at least 10. "Sir, Thelma mentioned that someone approached you about George. Did they need a working farm dog?"

"Thelma shouldn't be discussing my private business. Did she tell you about my overdue fines, as well?"

I laughed. "Nope, although I'd be happy to return your books for you. I was curious about George because someone's been trying to get their hands on Frost Gentry, as well."

"Maud's dog? Seemed like Frost just wanted a day off. Came over my fence like a gazelle and left again. Graceful girl, despite the surgical dressing."

"She's home now. But I can't rest until I know she'll stay safe. Maud is the breeder of my dog, as well, you see."

The door opened a bit more—enough for Percy to slip inside to do his routine inspection. If either Wendel or George noticed the cat, they didn't let on.

"I heard she bred prizewinners," Wendel said. "George has a few ribbons himself from his early days, when we had time for such frivolities."

"I'm sure you and Maud have plenty in common," I said.

"The main thing we have in common is that we don't mix. I value my privacy and she values hers. Plus, we're both newcomers to Thistledown." He snorted. "Anything under 10 years is a newcomer, it seems. I've got nine to go before I'm on the bottom rung of the social ladder. By that time I'll be as far under the grass as that lad, Kale Bibb."

"It can't be that bad," I said. "Thelma seems to have taken to you and she's rather selective."

His lip twitched. "Probably grateful someone still reads. There's nothing like holding a nice big book in your hands."

I took a wild guess. "Did you borrow the encyclopedia of dogs, by any chance? I saw it on her cart and wondered who else shared my passion for all things canine."

The door opened fully at last, and I saw he was dressed in a blue flannel shirt, dark jeans, and work boots his wife had probably wanted to retire.

"Had to wheel that one home in a wagon," he said, reaching down to pat his dog. "I was succession planning. Hope George is with me a while yet, but he's nearly 14. That's a good age for any dog."

"And what breed did you decide on after your research?" My smile was genuine now, and his was, too.

"Once you've had a border collie, there's no going back, I'm afraid. Would you agree?"

I nodded. "I can only hope Keats lives to be a good age like George."

He rubbed his free hand over his nearly bald head and a few strands of white hair lifted in the breeze. "I want George to enjoy the retirement he deserves. Owe him that and more. So when someone broke in here a week or so ago, I got pretty riled. The dog let me know. His hearing is shot but his nose works great."

Keats offered a proper bow to George and the older dog seemed to incline his head modestly.

"Did you get a look at the guy?" I asked.

"They got a look at my shotgun and ran out this very door like there were rockets under their sneakers."

"Plural? How many were there?"

"Two. One was Kale Bibb. The other wore a balaclava. Navy blue jacket."

"What makes you think they were after George?"

"Wieners. Dropped a pack in the hall, along with a leash." He shook his head. "As if George would throw me over for all-beef hotdogs. He'd have to be senile as well as deaf, which he isn't."

I stared down at the dog again, perplexed. "It seems strange to break in so brazenly to steal any dog."

"George isn't just any dog. Like I said, he's a prizewinner."

"I mean no disrespect, but you said yourself that George's best herding days are behind him."

Wendel leaned against the doorframe. "Never said his

ribbons were for herding. George was known for his scent work. I could only afford this house because he found a few treasures along the way. I bet that's what the thugs had in mind. Would never have worked, though. You can steal a dog but you can't make him hunt." The old man's voice was confident but his pale hands, lined with blue veins, twisted together. "I'd take extreme measures to protect my dog, young lady. But I didn't kill Kale Bibb, if that's what you think."

"The idea hadn't occurred to me, sir. Although I'd most certainly take extreme measures for mine, too."

"As it should be. The partnership between man and dog is sacred."

"Even when the man is a woman," I said, with a grin. "Mr. Barrick, someone took Kale out of commission and I'd like to do the same with his partner. Legally, I mean. There's a chance the balaclava guy is behind the crime and may have stolen Frost, too."

"Wish I could tell you more, but like I said, they left in a hurry. The cops didn't even bother to show up since nothing was stolen."

"Are you sure there's nothing else?" I gestured behind him. "Because my cat seems to think there's an item of interest here."

The old man and his deaf dog had missed the jangle of keys scraping toward us along hardwood, but Keats had gone into a point.

Wendel bent over to collect the key ring. He flipped through them and stopped abruptly. "There's one missing. The key to my old cabin. I kept a tract of land with our first house and small barn to preserve our memories. We raised our family there, and eight dogs, each wonderful in its own way."

"Would Kale have known about the cabin?" I asked.

He slipped the keys in his pocket and nodded. "Used to catch him and his sister stealing from my fruit trees and I never put them off. Knew they had a hard time at home. Their dad was a poor excuse for a man and an abomination as a father. If those kids wanted to make themselves sick on apples and peaches, I let them."

"No good deed goes unpunished," I said. "Is there a chance there's treasure buried on your land—or the property you sold?"

"Doubt it. George would have found anything like that long ago. He was better than ground penetrating radar. But those lads may have bought into the local legends. People think there's gold everywhere."

"I assume you'll tell Chief Harper all this when he visits?" I asked.

"Of course." Wendel tipped his head at me. "The police have their hands full for a bit. What do you say we take a drive out there and see what our dogs find?"

"I'd say you're on, Mr. Barrick. George, Keats and Percy could save the cops some time."

The old man put on his jacket and led the way to his pickup. "I heard about you and your crew, you know."

"I suppose Thelma showed you my file?" I said. "Never trust a librarian."

"Always trust a librarian," he corrected, opening the passenger door for me. "That credo has served me well."

I climbed in and buckled up. "I sensed you and I would become friends when I realized you'd borrowed the encyclopedia of dogs. I broke the spine on that book in Clover Grove. Overuse is one thing our librarian never complained about."

He glanced at me while closing the door. "I figure I can probably tolerate you because of the way your dog regards you."

I rolled down the window. "My chief goal in life is to earn that regard. It's priceless."

Wendel lifted George into the back seat and my pets joined the senior dog without a second thought.

I had second thoughts, however, when the old man pounded the gas just outside of town. Then he took a turn onto a side road and roared around a curve.

Percy let out a shriek of protest. It was an obvious warning—at least to me—but Wendel dismissed it.

"Cats," he grumbled, speeding up even more. "They have their place but it isn't on a sharp curve."

He didn't know my cat, though. Percy offered another yowl, but it was already too late.

CHAPTER TWENTY-FIVE

The specter of a blowout was something that haunted me. I'd woken many a night sweating and shaking after sending the truck careening off the road in my dreams. Somehow it had never happened.

Till now.

This time, it was very much real and just like my nightmares... only I wasn't behind the wheel.

And thank goodness for that, because Wendel Barrick knew how to handle a pickup in a crisis. Even so, we landed in a ditch.

After checking that the pets were okay, we sat staring at each other, a little dazed.

"Guess the cat was onto something," he said.

I managed a nod. "He usually is."

We got out and helped each other up the bank and onto the highway. About 20 yards behind us silver flecks glittered in the slanting rays of the sun.

"Nails," he said. "Deliberately scattered, most likely, since this is my side road. Normally I would have noticed. Got caught up in what's left of my testosterone."

Laughing, I patted his arm. "No harm done. Everyone's fine. But we're stuck."

He scanned the highway. "I can't change the tire from the ditch. Need to get the mechanic out and it'll take nearly an hour."

"How about I continue on foot and you meet me there?"

Wendel texted for help and then scanned the road and fields, probably hoping another solution would come to mind. When it didn't, he said, "No gentleman sends a lady into a dangerous situation alone. I'd rather you wait."

"I won't be alone," I said. "Keats and Percy are trained in warfare and you'll join us soon. I can call on my friends, but I don't want them hitting the same patch of nails."

His eyes brightened behind his glasses. "I have a metal detector and a magnet in the back so I can take care of that. The missus used to tease me about the stuff I carted around but it came in handy. You never know when disaster is going to strike."

"Two of my friends feel exactly the same way," I said. "I bet you have a bunker."

He gave a little nod. "There's someplace to hole up in case of emergency. That's why I held onto this tract of land. No room for a bunker in town."

Reaching out, I pumped his hand. "I'm so glad Thelma sent me your way, sir. You are one of my people."

That brought out a smile. "I appreciate that, considering I didn't listen to your cat and drove you into a ditch."

"Everything happens for a reason," I said, "although I hate it when people say that. Honestly, there is no good reason I can see for half the stuff that happens to me."

"Take George with you. He'll show you the fastest way to the old house."

George outright refused to leave his owner and the mixture

of frustration and gratitude on Wendel's face made me laugh again. "If someone's sprinkling nails on your road, Mr. Barrick, you need George for protection."

"Call me Wendel," he said. "And that's what a rifle's for. There's another, if you know how to fire one."

I shook my head. "I'll never be a good enough shot to keep my animals safe. They move fast and aren't always predictable."

We exchanged numbers and then Keats rounded me up with a mumble and headed back down into the ditch with Percy. "I guess this is the fastest route," I said, following.

"It is. Be careful, now. It's a bit of a hike, so I shouldn't be too far behind you. Stay in touch."

Just before I pushed into deep bush, I turned to wave. The old man was standing with a metal detector in one hand and a rifle in the other. He lifted the latter in a salute and I grinned over my luck. Another curious character to add to the beads on the string of my life. It got longer and more vibrant all the time, and it was part of the web that kept me safe and moving forward.

Keats grumbled that this was no time for reflection.

"Sure, it is. It's always the right time for gratitude. Look at all the great people we've met."

He mumbled again and I shrugged.

"I suppose we've met bad people in equal numbers, but the power of good outweighs the negative."

The next mumble was short. It sounded like, "Debatable."

"Yeah, I know. I just have to keep thinking that way or get bogged down. Let's focus on what we've accomplished here already. We have new friends in Maud and Louisa. You and Frost can have family reunions."

His next sound was a snort. A definite "whatever."

I laughed at that. "Family isn't easy, I grant you that. I had no clue about how difficult it would be to navigate all the landmines in my clan when I came home. Dad's family, Mom's family, my own brother and sisters... And I know that's not the end of it. So if you only have one sister to give you a run for your money, consider yourself lucky."

Much of the monologue that followed got lost in the bush between us and it was probably for the best. I caught the gist of it, which was that he liked being a class unto himself. A lone wolf, as it were. His younger sister thought too highly of herself for his liking.

I laughed again. "Maud infused both of you with confidence, and that's wonderful. No shrinking violets in your family. But I agree that you're in a class by yourself. There's no question in my mind."

He stopped walking and turned back to nudge my hand and give me a shot of warmth from his brown eye. Blatant affection was rare enough at any time, let alone during a mission. It was enough to worry me. "What's wrong, buddy?"

Already on the move again, he kept his thoughts to himself. We were getting closer to Wendel's home and Percy was the one to announce our arrival with a meow. It sounded like a greeting and as the woods opened to a clearing, I saw why.

Frost was sitting on a hillock, head back and pulling in loud snorts of air. When we emerged, she stood and offered a polite wag or two and then came down and circled to herd us. Despite the bandage, she didn't limp at all.

Keats took a little dash at her, teeth bared. He was not about to be herded by his baby sister on his own mission. There was only one leader here, and it was him.

"Stand down, Officer Keats," I said. "Frost, are you alone?"

Her higher-pitched mumble overlapped Keats' as they both tried to communicate with me.

"I'll take that as a yes. You slipped past everyone, including our personal security guard. Definitely no slouch in evasive maneuvers."

Pulling out my phone, I texted the news to Jilly. I also shared our location and a warning about the nails in the road.

Keats and Frost exchanged "words" that I couldn't quite translate. The sharp tone told me all I needed to know.

"Listen, you two. As hard as this might be to hear, you're both geniuses. Keats, your sister proved herself by escaping six people and finding us here, with nothing to go on as far as I know. She came to help you as much as me. And Frost, whatever your natural abilities, know that Keats has faced countless threats over the past couple of years. You have youthful exuberance and gifts of your own, but he has practical experience."

They continued to grumble, higher and lower pitches making both unintelligible. That's probably how it sounded to outsiders when I argued with my siblings. No one heard anyone else.

"Enough. I am counting on both of you to behave like team players. If you get caught up competing, you'll miss things. If you can't agree to agree, we will sit here until my human team arrives."

That simmered them both down pronto. They were alike in wanting to be first on the scene for any action.

Percy stared from one dog to the other and gave a hiss to underscore his contempt.

"There you have it," I said. "Don't ruin this for Percy, either. We can be stronger with another team member, or weaker. Your choice."

The dogs answered by coming together shoulder to shoulder behind Percy. For a second their fur actually touched and they sprung apart, as if stung. It made me snicker because that's how Asher and I had always behaved, despite being the closest kids in the family. Even now it was easier to shove than hug each other.

"Good. Onward. I see the roof of the barn through the trees. I didn't expect it to be so tall."

Wendel had described it as the "small barn," but it was bigger than mine at Runaway Farm. His large barn on the main property must have been a significant operation.

Percy stopped long before we reached it so that we could take in our surroundings. The barn was still in good condition. Beyond it sat a cabin that was old but well maintained. The property, however, was reverting to wilderness, just as it did throughout hill country if you turned your back for a second. I could see why Wendel and his wife had chosen to move into town for their final act.

I could also see how this site, and probably dozens of others in the area, would provide an ideal backdrop for the crime that also closed in on hill country when the police turned their backs for a second. Kellan and all his colleagues would have their hands full trying to whack it down like mole after mole in a dangerous game.

Percy was the first to bristle and Keats was close behind. Frost cast her green eyes sideways at her brother and then out-bristled him. Her brown ears flattened and her tail rose in a stiff flag. I wasn't sure if she was just competing, but the double dog display of hackles also doubled my wariness. It was good to know Wendel, and very likely Edna and Gertie, were on their way.

We were losing the sun faster than I expected. A bank of dark clouds gradually concealed the late afternoon rays I'd counted on to light our way. Checking my phone, I saw my battery was dwindling, too. One of my rules in any investigation was to keep a full charge but camping out at Maud's house had thrown me off my routine.

"We'll have enough power for a look around the house and barn," I murmured. "I'm already assuming from the hackles that someone's been holing up in one or the other. Are they here right now?"

Frost was the first to mumble a negative, earning a baleful glance from her brother. It was astounding how much she sounded like Keats. There wasn't a huge learning curve between us, which I appreciated. Coming off trying to understand songbirds, rabbits and parrots, this was a piece of cake.

That said, dogs were individuals and sibling sheepdogs were no exception. Their movements were similar, but Frost was faster and a little smoother in her gait. Keats stopped to lift his paw in a point to confirm that the barn was our destination, whereas Frost went on ahead. Then she circled back and tried to copy Keats, pointing at me, instead. He gave a pant-laugh, but I was impressed she was picking things up so quickly.

"Good girl," I whispered. "Let's be super careful. We'll do a quick reconnaissance and wait near the road for the others. If Kale's killer has been hanging around, he means business. Whatever his business might be."

Percy's soulful meow made me pause. I didn't always understand him the way I did Keats, but in this case, his tone made me look at my canine sidekick and then his sister. Was the killer's business really about the dogs? And how had Kale run afoul of him?

The barn door was locked, but Wendel had given me a second key he kept in the glove compartment of the truck. I found a pair of latex gloves in my pocket and pulled them on to avoid ruining any evidence Kellan might need later. Then I unlocked the door and drew it wide open to let in as much light as possible. The cloud cover obliged and withdrew at just the right moment to send strong beams inside.

I took it as a sign that fate was with us.

The dogs didn't seem fully convinced, however, and Percy most definitely thought otherwise. With a flash of bright eyes in my direction, the cat disappeared into the shadows within.

Keats fell back to my side despite what was probably a strong urge to keep up with his sister. Frost must have felt a shift however, because she turned and fell into the same position on my other side. I was flanked by two good dogs and felt more secure than usual in dubious circumstances.

I flicked on my phone light to supplement the waning sunlight and the three of us moved from pen to pen, searching for a sign of habitation. It seemed like the barn was going to be a bust until we reached the very last stall. High walls had likely held a horse at one time and I moved to the door to take a look inside.

Atop a deep pile of hay lay a sleeping bag. A large backpack stood in the corner and a navy windbreaker dangled from a hook in the wall. The jacket had a logo I recognized, and if I examined it further, I'd probably find a hole where Frost had torn the fabric.

The owner of the gear was nowhere to be seen but hopefully he'd put on another, heavier coat and gone on a nice, long hike. The dogs' hackles suggested he hadn't trekked nearly far enough. Maybe he was in Wendel's kitchen right now, cooking up a hearty meal.

I decided we wouldn't investigate the cabin after all. Maybe I was losing my nerve after pledging my troth to Kellan, but I just didn't feel great about this. Jilly would say I was finally developing some horse sense.

In a horse stall.

The thought made me snicker.

Kneeling, I rifled through the backpack. I took some photos and pocketed a few things to share with Kellan before they could vanish.

Keats silently nudged my calf to move on. A horse stall definitely wouldn't be my first choice for a confrontation. There would be little room to maneuver and climbing was never my strong suit, especially since injuring my ankle a couple of months ago. The ligaments had never had a chance to tighten up properly.

In fact, a twinge of discomfort when I stood made me question whether I'd just heard something creak in the distance. Had the others arrived already?

Both dogs circled from opposite sides and crossed behind me in a double herding arc. It would have amused me if my own hackles hadn't prickled.

The jacket's owner was closer now, I suspected. If we were destined to meet, I would prefer it to be outside, where there was more light and plenty of room to run.

Not that running would help me if he had a gun. I wondered how Kale had died. Why hadn't I thought to ask Kellan last night?

I let the dogs escort me out into the open area near the double doors and stopped in a patch of sunlight.

"Percy," I called. "Let's go."

"He's up here with me," someone called down from the hay loft. "Nice kitty."

CHAPTER TWENTY-SIX

A bolt of terror zipped from my scalp to my toes. The dogs pressed into my legs on opposite sides and my hands dropped to touch two sets of ears. I hoped the latex glove and rubber washer would hold my engagement rings in place if this situation came to blows.

And if the man was holding my cat hostage, it definitely could come to blows. I wasn't leaving without Percy.

"Hello," I called, tipping my head back. "Sorry to invade your privacy here. Just waiting for my cat and we'll be on our way."

"I'll send him right down," he said. There was a bloodcurdling yowl, followed by a yelp from the man.

The next scream came from me.

A fishing net with a long handle poked over the edge of the loft. An orange blob dangled from the webbing. If I had any doubt about the net's contents, Percy's string of feline curses confirmed his predicament. He had been snagged in the most undignified way.

"Pull my cat back to safety right now," I yelled up at the man.

I angled the phone light around but all I could see of him was the brim of a rust-colored baseball cap. It was enough to make me press record on my phone. Whatever he had to say, Kellan would likely want to hear.

"Sure." The guy's voice was deceptively genial. "I have no interest in the cat, other than trading him."

"Trading him? For what?" I asked, although I already knew.

"For the dog, of course." His laugh had the hollow sound of the soulless. The sociopathic. I had heard that sort of laugh often enough to know. It told me exactly what I was dealing with and just how hard I'd need to dance on my bum ankle until help arrived.

"That trade is not mine to make. Frost belongs to Maud Gentry and I've pledged to protect her."

"Knock yourself out." He gave that chilling laugh again. "No, seriously. Knock yourself out and save me the trouble. She's not the dog I want, anyway. The other one's yours to give."

My heart had already been struggling to settle back into a normal rhythm and now it seemed to stutter and stagger in my chest. Keats poked my fingers to get me to focus. I tried, but there were spots before my eyes and only half of them were dust motes. Something thick and heavy like wool clogged my throat.

"Don't go getting all emotional," the man said. His words suggested he could see more of me than I could of him. "It's just a dog."

I shook my head far too hard, but at least the movement cleared my eyes and throat. "That's where you're wrong. He's not just a dog. He's my heart."

The voice didn't sound like mine but the sentiment did.

"See, that's your emotions talking. Typical of childless women your age. You've projected baby cravings onto your pets."

Rage filled my chest and that kicked my heart—and hopefully my brain—back into gear. He wasn't wrong about baby cravings, but I had plenty of emotional capacity available for my animals. There was no need to project anything.

"You'll feel the same one day," I said, standing on tiptoe to try to get a look at him. I had my suspicions but wanted visual confirmation. "From what I hear, it takes men a little longer to give in to their daddy cravings."

He laughed again. "That won't happen. I don't have the right lifestyle to raise a family."

"I suppose not, when you're dangling cats over ledges like that. It doesn't bode well for raising a child."

"Your cat's fine. It's a strong net. Frost can tell you, since you two get along so well."

The dog shivered under my left hand and I felt my rings slip to my knuckle despite the latex. My fingers had turned icy and shriveled. I hadn't really thought about that when I delayed getting them properly fitted.

"She escaped, though," I said. "And it looked like she took a chunk of you with her."

"A small one," he admitted. "And your cat took another just now."

"Have you got enough flesh to spare for my own dog? What'll be left for the kids Sunny Bibb's dreaming of having with you someday soon?"

A pause and a noticeable shift in energy told me I'd guessed right. The man I'd seen on her photo roll was the one holding my cat hostage.

"She can keep dreaming," he said. "Because that'll never happen. She was only a means to an end."

"Her brother's end, poor thing. You used her to get to him."

It was a fishing expedition, and a diversion to move under the net. If he dropped Percy, I would do my very best to catch him and hope the cat's nine lives did the rest. I wasn't sure how many remained after our previous exploits.

"I know you think you're pretty smart, but you got that wrong. Sunny just fell for my obvious charms."

My laughter sounded a bit strangled but it still passed for amusement. "And so she gave you the key to her mother's place and you stole Frost."

"Still wrong. Well, I borrowed the key from her but Sunny wasn't part of it. Her idiot brother insisted on that."

I never knew Kale Bibb yet it somehow made me happy to know he hadn't thrown his family under a bus.

"You got the key. You got the dog. Why did you kill him?" I asked.

There was a long pause and I knew he was calculating. He wanted to answer but only if he was sure he could take me out after telling me. If he confirmed, it would reveal a lot about his intentions. And his confidence.

"Because he got cold feet about breaking into his mother's place," he said at last. "I needed the dog and Kale wanted to protect his family. He became a hindrance so I had to remove him from the equation."

The confession likely meant this guy was quite sure he could kill me and *not* kill my dog. Since we could easily get outside before he climbed down from the loft, he probably had a gun and a good eye.

I signaled for Keats and Frost to leave but they defied me. As I expected, although I'd hoped otherwise.

"You needed Frost so much you'd kill Kale? Why?"

"To get to the real prize, obviously. I knew if we snagged your dog's sister, the breeder would bring you down here. Everyone knows about you and what that dog can do."

"Dalton, you don't know dogs very well. My border collie

won't work for anyone but me. Or occasionally my police chief fiancé. Keats won't even work for his breeder."

There was another long pause. "How did you learn my name?"

"I remember you from Mandy's Country Store in Clover Grove. You almost ran into us coming down the stairs. When she said you were asking questions, I snapped a pic and got the chief to run your plates. I collect information just in case I need it someday, like a magpie gathers pretty stones. Then I saw your photo on Sunny's phone and it looked vaguely familiar. All the strands came together a few minutes ago. Except for one thing."

He didn't want to ask, but like most sociopaths, ego drove him to it. "What thing?"

"Why *my* dog? What makes him worth murdering someone for?"

The net holding Percy slid back from the open space over my head and I followed, until the orange fluff disappeared into the depths of the loft. I didn't feel much relief because my cat's captor could just as easily hurl him over the edge, or do something much worse.

In fact, his actions likely signaled an escalation and I needed to stall him as long as I could.

"Dalton?" I said. "I know you're going to kill me anyway. You might as well satisfy my curiosity and tell me why you want my dog."

"It's not about your dog, per se. They want your dog because they want *you*. Apparently you're a package deal."

"They want *me*? Why?"

Finally his face appeared over the edge. It was indeed the handsome man who'd passed us on the stairs at Mandy's after burying Kale among the other victims in Clover Grove. He wasn't a prince but an emotional pauper.

"If you need to ask, you're not as smart as they think. Right now, you're an impediment to their work. A thorn in their side. And you need to be neutralized."

I stood under him, staring up. "Neutralized? I suppose that means shot?"

His shoulders moved in what I assumed was a shrug. "Dead or alive, I'll get paid. You decide."

He pulled back long enough for me to send the recording to Kellan. Then I held the phone over my head to light up his next move. If he wanted to shoot me, I was an easy target.

But it wasn't a gun that came over the edge.

He unfurled something that looked like a large blanket and then dropped it.

Now I was the one netted like a fish.

CHAPTER TWENTY-SEVEN

His aim was remarkably good, considering a cat had landed on his head to knock off the baseball cap and deliver an 18-claw massage. The thick, heavy gauge net knocked me right off my feet and I fell to the floor on my side. Squirming and thrashing as I tried to flip onto my back, I only seemed to tangle myself more.

Then my fingers touched fur through the net and I realized Keats was stuck, too. My inner switch flipped from panic to wrath, and I slowed down to concentrate. Thrashing wasn't getting me anywhere. I needed to be deliberate about my movements and take advantage of the reprieve Percy was giving us. Every minute brought help closer, either Wendel Barrick and his rifle, or Edna and Gertie with their arsenal. Or even the police, if I was very lucky. All I had to do was get myself out of this trap, rescue the pets and run for my life. And theirs.

The first step toward freedom was simply flipping onto my back and facing my opponent.

Only it wasn't simple at all. The net was so heavy that I wondered if it was meant to snare a rhino. I hoped it wasn't lined with wire because I intended to use tooth and claw to get out.

One breath, two breaths... On the third, I pushed up from the floor, remembering the upper body strength I'd built through hard farm labor. When there was enough slack, I shoved even harder, cleared the floor and twisted.

I didn't quite make it, but close enough. A bit of strategic squirming got me onto my back, staring up through a lattice of fiber. It was so dense I felt like I was smothering, even though there were plenty of gaps.

A mumble beside me told me to focus. There was a note in the message I'd never heard before. Suppressed panic. Despite all his many resources, Keats couldn't get out of this literal bind. When I turned my head slightly, I saw that he was compressed into a small black-and-white mound in the web dropped by the toxic spider above. He'd applied his teeth diligently to create a small hole but at this rate, it would take ages. Percy could only hold Dalton off so long no matter how many feline lives were left in his bank.

More weight landed on my midriff and bright eyes looked down at me. Frost had either been out of the line of fire or dodged the net just in time.

"Run, Frost," I said. "Go get help."

Her shrill mumble delivered a clear message. She was going nowhere without us.

"All right, then. Chew! Get Keats out and work together."

She did as I asked. My phone was somewhere nearby casting a circle of light and I saw white canine teeth flashing as both dogs gnawed. The weight of the fiber told me it would be slow going even for two. At best we probably had five minutes while Percy did his thing and kept the guy from reaching the ladder to come down and join us. The man's screaming told me the cat was giving it his all.

At least I knew Dalton Park likely wasn't going to shoot me. When someone said "dead or alive," I figured alive paid better. His boss or colleagues wanted something from me—likely information on what the police knew or didn't know about the current state of criminal affairs in our region. They would assume my fiancé confided in me about such things. And they would be wrong. I had little intel to give and it was clear they had no compunction about dispatching people who stood in their way. Worse, they'd have no compunction about dispatching pets to torture information out of me first.

Good luck to them. It would only make me fight harder.

Starting now.

Reaching into my front pocket, I pulled out the knife I'd pilfered from my assailant's backpack. It was much bigger and sharper than my pocketknife and sliced through the netting like butter. I wanted to free Keats first, but the flashes of fur and teeth from both dogs told me I'd struggle to use the knife without drawing blood until I got a better angle.

I slashed an X about 18 inches long and wide. It was enough of a gap to deliver myself back into an ugly world of terror.

As I sat up, head and shoulders free, the man stopped moving long enough to shine a flashlight down and assess my status.

I expected him to run to the ladder to take back the advantage before I freed Keats.

Instead, he did something far more dramatic.

With Percy still on his head, he stuck the light in his pocket and then grabbed a long heavy rope that was tied to the rafters. Wrapping both arms and one leg around it, he used the other leg to shove off from the ledge. He swung out over the wide space, yelling like Tarzan.

The screech wasn't for effect: Percy had clearly dug in to survive the ride.

I was terrified for my cat and also terribly proud of him. There was no time to admire his courage under pressure, however. I had work to do.

Panic propelled me to my feet and I bent to move Frost aside. She was in such a frenzy that she nearly nipped me and then mumbled an apology.

"It's okay, girl. Just let me finish."

Yanking on the net, I pulled it up and away from Keats so that I could slash it. We were nearly there.

"Stay still, buddy. Just one more second."

That second was our undoing.

Dalton swung back on his jungle vine, lowering himself with apelike dexterity. Before I could pull the knife more than a couple of inches, he hit me with far more than the full force of his 200 pounds and grabbed me with one arm. The floor fell away as he carried me across the barn and then used me as a human shield when he hit the wall.

At a guess, I dropped about eight feet and landed on my side with a thud that knocked the wind out of me.

Dalton swung back yet again and let go of the rope when he was right over the dogs.

I sucked in a sharp and painful breath, praying he wouldn't land on them. Perhaps he wanted to, but his aim was off because Percy had wrapped his furry body around the man's face, either through genius or desperation.

Using both hands, Dalton pried the cat off. That handsome face would bear deep scars from Percy's handiwork—a reminder of this episode that would stay with him for decades.

Unless I killed him now.

For the first time, as I saw him hurl Percy aside and reach for Keats, I felt capable of true violence. Dalton was after my dog—the canine love of my life—and I would show no mercy.

All I needed was something to do the job. The knife had

slipped from my fingers as I fell. Scrambling to my feet, I looked around for it.

Frost ran toward me with the handle in her jaws. She dropped the knife on my boots. I grabbed it and we turned together to face our opponent. "Let's get him," I said.

My scream, her howl and Percy's yowl overlapped in a harrowing sound.

Dalton was moving toward the door with Keats in his arms. The net that still bound my dog had turned him into a powerless ball and diminished him to a mere 40 pounds of fur. Normally he added another 40 pounds of fighting fury to that.

Percy jumped first, landing mid-back and clinging there, delivering his massage between the man's shoulder blades.

This time Dalton didn't even yell. He was probably pumped so full of adrenaline and determination that he didn't even feel it.

Frost went after him, yanking on one pant leg and then the other.

It barely slowed the guy down. He was like a machine. The Terminator.

The weight of the net seemed like nothing more than cobwebs to him. As he moved through the double doors, he twisted it up and slung the loose end over his shoulder, knocking Percy off again.

I followed Dalton outside as fast as wobbly legs could carry me. The knife was in my raised hand and I was determined to use it to liberate my dog.

The main barrier now was dusk. During the skirmish inside, the sun had set, dropping a blanket of darkness that seemed heavier than the net.

My phone was in the barn, shining a light uselessly, whereas I was out here struggling to follow over rocky terrain Dalton knew much better than I did.

Keats mumbled encouragement to me, which seemed to remind Dalton he was human, or something approximating it. "Shut up, dog, or I'll use my gun on her."

"Stop," I called. "You want me, not the dog. So put him down. I surrender."

This time Keats' whine was high enough pitched that perhaps only Frost and I heard it. She was still nipping Dalton's calves and hauling at his cuffs. It would have slowed an ordinary man but this guy was far from that.

"Change of plans," he said. "The dog's a better option."

At least he was puffing. It wasn't quite as easy as he made it look.

He went around the side of the barn, gaining so much ground I could only see his outline from the bit of light that shone through his pocket. Percy ran ahead, orange tail lashing and guiding me. I stumbled along a twisting gravel path lined with stones big enough to turn my ankle if I didn't tread carefully.

Up ahead, there was a high-pitched yelp I knew to be Frost's, and another infuriated growl that came from Keats.

Then came a metallic slam, scuffling sounds and another shrill yelp from Frost. He had kicked her, I suspected.

Keats' howls were muffled now. He'd been contained. Trapped. Probably a sheepdog's worst nightmare and certainly mine.

"Stop," I called again. "I'll come with you. Tell you every-thing you want to know. And I know a lot."

"We'll be in touch," he called back.

A motor turned over. It sounded like an ATV that was smaller than Edna's but big enough to handle this landscape. The headlight that came on showed me I was right. There was a box at the back that no doubt held my most precious possession. As the vehicle moved forward, the net dragged behind like a long wedding veil, snagging on rocks and tearing as Dalton relentlessly rolled on.

Percy had become a blurry flash of orange, in hot pursuit, somehow managing once more to land on the guy's back. The last thing I saw as they crested a hill was Dalton swatting at my cat.

Frost circled back for me, wailing as Keats never had before. She seemed torn between going after the ATV and protecting me. Perhaps my need for her to pursue conflicted with Keats' order to stay. I could understand how difficult it was to be caught between us, quite literally.

"It's okay," I said. "We'll go after them together. See the lights down the road? Our friends are nearly here. We just need to figure out where he's driving and everyone will help. We'll get Keats back."

The reassurance was more for me than Frost. There was no way she could come anywhere close to the level of attachment I felt for my dog—not to mention the cat riding along. But she felt my distress, and probably knew well that her owner would be heartbroken, too.

We ran together, the dog just ahead of me, the white tip of her tail showing me the way. The ATV idled for a second, perhaps assessing if we still pursued, and then the headlight went out.

I could still see the faint glow of Dalton's pocketed flashlight and the noisy motor was easy enough to follow. But he left the trail, trundling over larger rocks, and then rolled down a hill. My legs pumped hard, despite the bum ankle, as I tried to keep up with Frost. Every so often a whine penetrated my panic. It came from Keats, not Frost, although I knew it was technically impossible for me to hear him over that motor, especially as it gained more distance. Yet I heard it nonetheless in my head. It seemed like he was trying to tell me something using our special connection.

Watch your step.

Watch your step.

Was that it? In all of this, what he wanted was for me to watch my step?

A second later, I understood why as the ground shifted under me and I dropped into utter darkness.

CHAPTER TWENTY-EIGHT

I was probably only unconscious for a few minutes before a bright light shone overhead and showed me I'd fallen into a cavern.

Make that a bunker.

"She's around here. Why can't this dog do a decent point like her brother? We don't have all night, dagnabit."

"Edna." My voice was weak. Frail. The sound of someone who'd nearly given up. "Edna, I'm here."

My friend may not have heard me but Frost managed to convey the message. "Ow! Stop that, you cur."

"We're close," someone else said. A man. "It's right around here."

I tried to place the voice. Not Asher. Not Kellan.

Kellan.

I wanted Kellan.

He would make all this right for me. Find my dog. Shoot Dalton Park. We could bury that loser in the gangster graveyard, and no one would be any the wiser.

"Give me the light," the man said again. "George found it."

I remembered now. It was Wendel Barrick and his sheep-dog, George.

"Here," I called, a little more forcefully now. I was down, no question, but I was not out. While there was breath in my body, I'd stand and fight for my dog.

The only problem was that I couldn't seem to stand or even sit up. Was I buried under rubble? Paralyzed?

A very bright light hit me square in the face.

"What's wrong with you, Ivy Rose Galloway? Lying around in a bunker when there's work to be done. Sit up, dagnabit."

Using my elbow, I propped myself up and then collapsed again. "Probably cracked a rib," I said. "Hurts to breathe."

I couldn't breathe. There was nothing left in my chest after my heart was ripped out.

"Is that whining?" Edna said. "Soldiers don't whine." Her voice faded as she spoke to someone else. "Give me the rope. I can hoist her out if her spine's not broken."

"It's not broken." I could feel my toes now. "Is Percy there? Is he all right?"

"Oh, thank goodness," Jilly said. "If she's asking about Percy, she's okay. Ivy, he's fine. Percy is fine."

"He took Keats. Jilly, he took Keats." I wanted to cry but couldn't. "On the ATV. Please go after him."

"Kellan and Asher are doing just that," she called down. "I'll tell them. Don't worry."

Wendel's face appeared in the opening. "I know this land far better than anyone except George. We'll nail that guy, young lady. You just focus on getting out of my bunker." He added more quietly, "There's a full medical kit inside. Including a spinal board."

"A man after my own heart," Edna said. "Good luck out there, Wendel."

"Save the flirting," I said. "At least until my dog is safe."

"That's better," Gertie said. "She's getting her spark back."

I wasn't, but the only way I'd find my spark was to get my dog back and for that I needed to get out of this hole. Why was there always a bunker waiting to swallow us up? I may have caught Dalton if this cave hadn't caught me.

There was a mumble up above. Familiar, yet not. Frost.

"I might have," I told her.

She mumbled back. It sounded like, "You wouldn't. It's better this way."

"Stop chitchatting with my dog and save your strength," Maud said.

"Ivy's going to be a hot mess," Louisa said. "I'm calling an ambulance."

"I'm good," I said, managing to push myself up this time. If I didn't get moving, they'd sideline me when I got above ground, and nothing was keeping me from going after Keats.

Frost mumbled that she'd join me.

"You're staying leashed," Maud said.

"Maud's right, Frost," I called. "They want you, too. Better to leave it to Wendel."

"But they want George, as well," Jilly said. "Or so he told us as we came in. What's with the dog grab?"

"Wendel has a rifle and more," Edna said, camo legs and boots now dangling into the bunker's entrance. "Won't hesitate to use weapons of force. Nor will Chief Fiancé."

"Can you get me out of here, Edna? Please?"

"Thought you'd never ask." She rappelled down into the cavern while Gertie made sure she was properly roped off, and Jilly and Louisa shone high-powered lights inside.

Dalton's trapeze ride in the barn might have added to my stockpile of trauma, but Edna was countering the negative vision with a positive one. Somehow, I even found a smile as my personal commando swung in.

She checked me over quickly and declared me safe for transport. Winding the rope around me, she created a makeshift swing and there were grunts from above as they hauled me up.

"Better ease up on the pie," Edna called after me. "Gertie and I are fit but there are limits."

"Pie," I said. "I could use some pie right about now. Strawberry rhubarb."

Jilly's expression changed from relief to concern. "Ivy, did you hit your head?"

Peeling off the latex gloves, I rubbed my fingers through my hair and found a tender spot, tacky with blood. "Nope. Just bruised some ribs."

It wasn't like me to lie to my best friend. Or to hide blood from her by wiping it on my overalls. But if she thought I was concussed again, there was no way she'd let me join the hunt for Keats. I was stubborn, but when it came to my health, she was more stubborn still.

"You wouldn't talk about pie if your faculties were intact," she said, directing a flashlight right into my face. "Besides, you hate rhubarb."

"Too close to a vegetable, right?" I shielded my face from the light. "I'm just joking around to prove I'm fine. So we don't waste time. Let's get going."

"Are you forgetting something?"

The voice came from the hole, where Edna was still waiting for us to hoist her up.

"Of course not," I said. "Edna, I need you to blow this jerk off the face of the earth for me."

"She's got competition," Gertie said, patting Minnie. "Nothing I hate more than a petnapper."

Jilly sat me down on a rock and joined the others to haul Edna up. I was secretly glad of the reprieve and even stayed there, with Percy under one arm and Frost, the other. "You two were awesome," I said. "Percy, you could star in your own movie but no one would ever believe you do your own stunts. And Frost, what you did with that knife was—"

"A knife?" Maud said, between groans as she pulled. "My dog had a knife?"

"She helped me escape a net and nearly got Keats free, too. That dog is a hero like her brother."

"I didn't want to find out that way." Maud's voice came more easily because Edna was out and on her feet.

"Let's carry Private Galloway to the van," Edna said.

"Carry me! Are you kidding? I refuse." I stood up and the arm holding Percy fell limply to my side. Luckily most of his claws were still operational because he dug in around my hip and then climbed to my shoulder.

"I saw that," Jilly said. "Something's wrong."

"Nothing's wrong except that my ribs hurt and my dog is missing."

Edna came over and briefly shone a small penlight into my eyes. "I don't think she's concussed, Jillian. Just in shock."

"She's going to the closest ER to get checked out," Jilly said.

"Not a chance. I won't go anywhere except after my dog."

Holding my shoulders, Edna stared at me with eyes that were both fierce and kind. "Private Galloway. You need to learn when to leave matters in expert hands."

"Sorry, Edna. I will not leave Keats behind. Besides, I'm totally fine. Obviously I'd be crying or fainting or worse if I were anything but fine."

"You're sweating," Edna said. "On a cold night."

I rubbed my forehead with trembling hands. "I'm a little stressed. Obviously."

"Stressed enough to be rubbing blood around your face," she said. "As the squad's medic, I'm sidelining you from action."

Slipping out from under her hands, I started to run. She

caught up with me easily and Gertie was close behind. Four hands clamped down on me and now I did start to cry.

"I'm sorry, Ivy, but no one's going to tell you which way they went," Gertie said. "Get in my van and go home with Maud so that Edna and I can join them. You're just slowing us down."

"Trust us," Edna said. "Have we let you down before?"

I shook my head, suddenly becoming aware of the pounding behind my eyes. "Okay. Okay. I give up."

Looping my arms through Jilly's and Louisa's, I walked meekly to the van and then slid into the passenger seat. Once Maud was behind the wheel and the back doors closed on the others, I slipped out again and ran.

Edna was right that I didn't know where Dalton had gone. But Percy did, and he was with me. As was Frost.

I had every reason to believe I would have found them... if the world hadn't gone suddenly black again.

CHAPTER TWENTY-NINE

A soft pillow slipped out from under my head and my temple clunked against cool glass. It felt nice. Too nice.

I had to wake up. There was something to do. Something desperately important.

A little nip on the back of my right hand confirmed it. I tried to move my hand, to steal a few more minutes of blissful sleep, but another nip followed. And another.

The fingers of my left hand found fluff, but I already knew who to blame. Keats delivered a bigger nip but Percy's was sharper. Surgical. It cut through nearly anything, including the sleep of the wounded and weary.

Keats. He was gone. Stolen. Netted like a carp and ferried away in the most humiliating of ways. My proud dog deserved far better and I couldn't give it to him because I was here sleeping, with my head bumping against glass and a cat biting my hand hard enough to kill a mouse.

"Ow! Percy, would you mind?"

"You're awake. Good! I don't know why the cat had to come with us, but he insisted."

My eyes finally opened and stared at a black police toque through the grill between the seats. Anger flared in my stomach. They'd put me in the back like a common criminal.

"Where are we going, Asher?" I asked.

"The closest emergency room. The only ambulance in the region is out on call so you're getting special delivery."

"It's a waste of time when we could be looking for my dog. I'm fine."

"No offense, sis, but you sure didn't look fine passed out in the field. Kellan nearly had a heart attack. Never seen him so upset before."

I was glad I missed that, actually. If there was anything left of my heart it didn't need to be shredded further. Touching my chest, I was relieved to feel the outline of my phone in my bib pocket. Someone had retrieved it from the barn and hopefully there was a little charge left.

"The pain from my ribs made me faint, that's all." I ran my fingers along Percy's back to stay grounded. "There's nothing you can do but muscle through it, right? You cracked ribs playing football."

"And hockey," he said. "My rec league is full of buffoons who like to take the cop down, but I give as good as I get."

"Your game was tonight. I'm sorry you're missing it."

"Like I'd ever put sports before family." He turned and the dashboard lit up his profile. He had the best features of both Mom and Dad, or at least had been born with them. Baseball had been hardest on his nose and it was a little crooked now. "Don't forget my wife's back there, stumbling around in an unfamiliar forest."

"I haven't forgotten." There were a lot of people looking for my dog and the man who absconded with him. The regional police had come out in force now, having been rallied by Kellan.

More officers had arrived from Clover Grove and even Dorset Hills.

I wasn't sure how I knew that because I remembered almost nothing after jumping out of Gertie's van and collapsing.

"It's going to be fine," my brother said. "There's no way that scumbag can know the terrain better than the cops."

I had my doubts about that. "Is Wendel Barrick still there? With George, his sheepdog? They know the terrain better than anyone."

Asher turned his eyes back to the road and nodded. "Plus the other sheepdog. She's no slouch either, apparently. They divided up in three parties and fanned out. I bet they found Keats already."

They hadn't. My phone would be pinging. His phone would be pinging. There was ominous silence, unless you counted the chatter on the police radio. Asher reached over and turned down the volume, likely worried I'd hear something that alarmed me. It probably wouldn't at this point. I was numb. Empty. Like I'd never feel anything again.

"Did Edna give me something for the pain?" I asked. "Because my ribs feel pretty good, now."

"Nope. Said you needed to suck it up like a soldier. Normally she'd be itching to use her hypodermic kit." A shudder passed over his shoulders, probably recalling Edna's school vaccination program. "She didn't want you to leave in the end. Kellan and Jilly insisted. They said you were talking gibberish."

"Well, you can tell I'm good, brother. No gibberish now. How about we turn around?"

"No can do. Direct orders from the chief." He chuckled. "My two chiefs."

"All right then. Let's get this over with. The hospital will tell you I'm fine and we can go back."

He nodded again. "You just rest and I'll text them you're doing great."

Doing great? Seriously? I was dead inside. Dogless. How could that in any way constitute greatness? Merely being alive didn't count for much. Without Keats I'd be useless to anyone else. I'd just keep searching for him and merely subsist until I found him. It was all my fault and I'd never get over the guilt and grief.

Fiddling with my engagement rings, I considered taking them off. I couldn't marry Kellan now. I would only be half a person. Less than half. It wasn't fair to him. But it also wasn't fair to lose the rings. Eventually he'd find someone whole and start over. They'd probably fit her finger perfectly, without the rubber washer. I was the wrong Cinderella after all. He'd been duped.

Another mile passed and some of the numbness receded. Percy sat on my lap purring as hard as he could. It was comforting, even if I didn't want to be comforted. The vibrations traveled through my legs and up my fingertips and suddenly a clear thought formed in my muddled mind.

He's alive. He's waiting. Don't give up.

Normally a thought bubble like that would come from Keats himself, but this spoke of him in the third person. It had a different tone to it. More compassionate. When I was indulging in self-pity, as I undoubtedly was now, Keats was curt. Even snippy. That's what he normally deemed necessary to get me moving in the right direction. It was a sheepdog herding nip to the ego.

This was a kinder, gentler prodding but it felt like herding nonetheless.

Frost.

It was the feminine version of Keats. Was she communicating with me over all these miles? If so, she was a very gifted dog indeed.

I felt something at my shin and reached down, expecting to find Asher's hockey stick or equipment.

Instead, I touched a warm nose. For the merest second I thought it was Keats. Then I decided it was a delusion—a figment from my addled brain.

I was wrong on both counts. A flash of a streetlight showed me a nose all right. This one was brown rather than black. Frost had apparently managed to slip into the police SUV and hide under my brother's parka. That's probably why Percy had created such a fuss about coming. It was a diversion.

The cat's purr amped up another notch and he started kneading my legs. Time to make a new plan. These pets hadn't gone to such lengths only to have me sit around moping. They were counting on me. Keats was counting on me even more. No one could save him but me, I figured. We had a flawless track record and I wasn't about to break it.

Percy meowed and pricked my legs through my overalls. There were fewer than 18 claws now, but they'd grow back. We were nothing if not resilient.

"Gotcha," I said.

Asher dropped his phone. "What was that, sis?"

"Just coughing a little. Can you wind down the window and give me some fresh air?"

"No. You're a flight risk."

"I'm a faint risk. Please. It's either fresh air or smelling salts."

He pondered for a minute then cracked the front passenger window. "More please," I said. "It's helping to clear my head."

The back and forth continued till the window was just over halfway down and he drew the line. How he expected me to get through the grill and hurl myself out onto the highway, I didn't know.

"I'm hungry," I said. "Can we stop for a burger?"

"A burger?" His voice was incredulous. "No, we can't stop for snacks. Straight to the ER. Do not pass go. The chief was clear."

"Ash, come on. Kellan wouldn't want me to starve, would he? I didn't get dinner."

He turned again and scanned me. "The Ivy I know wouldn't want to eat at a time like this."

"You've got your sisters mixed up. This Ivy always wants to eat. If there was pie, I'd take it. Preferably Mandy McCain's coconut cream. What's your favorite pie, brother?"

"Forget it. I know how you work. I'm not falling for your decoys."

"If I'm as addled as everyone says, how could I pull the pie over your eyes? I'm just passing time with pleasant conversation. But I'll get more insistent if we pass a burger joint."

"Tell you what," he said. "I'll bring you the finest meal the hospital has to offer on a silver platter. Once you're cuffed to a stretcher."

"Okay. Be that way."

I had no idea where we were right now. It was pitch black, aside from lights placed so far apart that we needed the high beams. Still, I pictured a burger in my head, whether the thought was my own, Frost's or even Asher's. My brother did love a hamburger.

Less than a mile later, a neon sign flashed a welcome from the roadside. "Buck Burgers," it read, with a dollar sign and the numeral one on the logo.

Asher pressed the pedal, hoping I wouldn't notice.

"It'll take five minutes, tops," I said. "We get a couple of burgers, buck apiece, and we're on our way."

"I've got a policy about eating meat that only costs a buck," he said.

"That's Jilly's policy, and normally it's a good one. But I'm the injured party here, and my stomach wants a buck's worth of beef right now. Brother, how often do I ask you for anything?"

He shook his head. "A lot. More than all my other sisters combined."

"That's because I'm your favorite, and you know it. You can't let me starve back here. And worse, I need to use the restroom. Please don't make me suffer the indignity of walking into the ER soiled."

The car slowed and I knew the threat of incontinence had prevailed. My brother had a queasy stomach that could handle cheap meat but not manure in any form.

"Ivy, if you pull any stunts here, I will take you down. Don't think I will be too embarrassed to tackle my own sister in public. I won't. At one time I might have been but I'm bucking for a promotion now. To make Jilly proud. And it won't come if I let the chief's fiancé do something stupid at Buck Burgers."

"We get in, we get out," I said. "I hit the loo while you place the order. Then I eat in silence back here till we get to the ER."

"Silence? You promise? Because when your lips are flapping, I start doubting the reality I see before me. You're twisty."

"I had to be. As the youngest Galloway, twisty was the only way to get a buck's worth of anything."

"Okay. Deal." He eased off the highway and onto the shoulder. "But only because I'm glad you're alive. Even alive and mouthy."

"Stick a burger in it and we're good," I said, as he got out and unlocked the door for me. He clicked the lock as we crossed the pavement. There were a couple of cars in the lot between us and the door.

Good.

I asked him to order me a basic burger and fries before heading to the restroom. Once inside, I texted him a few specifics. Extra cheese. No mustard. Double relish. Half a dill pickle, thinly sliced. Tomato, seedless. Bacon, extra crispy. A tablespoon of chopped onion. And cracked pepper.

When I was done, I waited a beat and texted, "Two of those, please. And a mint chocolate chip shake. Hold the chocolate chips."

The list would have been enough to blow the fair hair clear off my brother's head at the best of times. I knew he'd have no choice but to read it aloud to the server and it would embarrass him greatly. I also knew he'd do it because he felt sorry for me.

Coming out of the restroom, I watched his reflection in the glass. He was leaning across the counter showing his phone to a tall skinny guy in a Buck Burgers T-shirt as they deciphered my order together.

Perfect.

I slipped out the front door and ran to the police SUV. A couple of teens in the next car were more entranced with each other than their burgers and they didn't look up as I passed.

My ribs barely hurt now, thanks to a good hit of adrenaline, although I certainly did notice them as I forced myself headfirst into the passenger seat. It was a very tight squeeze and I wouldn't have made it if I hadn't taken my coat off first and fed it inside.

"Nothing to it," I grunted, clambering into the driver's seat. "At least, if my brother is as predictable as I think." I groped around under the driver's seat and found it: a small, rusted metal box that held mentholated cough drops about 70 years ago. It belonged to my delinquent grandfather on the Galloway side and my father had one just like it under the seat of his truck. Asher had lost enough keys over the years that he took no chances. Maybe there was another one hidden underneath the vehicle. Magnets glued to the back kept the boxes in place.

I stuck the key in the ignition and kept the lights off as I eased the police SUV out from between the parked cars and then rolled rather quickly onto the highway.

Checking the rearview mirror, I saw my brother standing outside the front door with a takeout bag in one hand. The other churned his hair and then pumped a fist in my direction. He was yelling and I hoped the young couple in the next car didn't stop making out long enough to film the tirade.

Slowing for a second, I flashed the lights once and gave the horn a tap. It seemed like the polite thing to do after hood-winking a good man.

CHAPTER THIRTY

A couple of miles down the road I pulled onto the shoulder and got out to let the dog and cat into the front seat.

"You know where we're going, right?"

A mumble and a meow offered confirmation.

"Maybe I should ask Wendel to meet up with us," I said, pulling out my phone. "It would be a help to have George along."

Frost's next mumble sounded more animated but I wasn't sure how to read her, yet. I'd have to do my best to interpret her vocal repertoire and actions. As similar as the dogs were, she wasn't Keats. We didn't have a finely-honed communication system. But we'd learn, and quickly, too.

"The problem is that if only you two know where we're going, I can't tell Wendel. So when you can give me a sign, I'll text him."

We got back on the road and I settled in. There were bells and whistles in the car I didn't recognize and I hoped I wouldn't need to use any of them. Still, it felt good to be piloting a police car down the road. Surprisingly good, considering I'd never been the type of person who cared about vehicles at all. Driving was a rite of passage for any country teen, but after leaving for college, I'd never bought a car, preferring to rent one on the rare occasions I needed to go anywhere. Jilly was the same and had barely driven in Clover Grove during our tenure.

Still, I was happy I'd mastered the truck and even Mom's car, balky old Buttercup, because it made driving the police vehicle less daunting. The SUV had an automatic transmission and drove like a dream.

"Nice ride, eh?" I asked my passengers.

My confidence tank refilled faster than I expected, thanks to the squad car. For the past two days, a sociopath had been messing with me in the worst possible way. He'd stolen my dog, deliberately run me into a bunker and left me for dead.

Now I would ride back in style to face him. He'd end up behind the grill, if I had anything to say about it. No burgers for Dalton.

Frost mumbled and her voice sounded more like Keats, only gentler. "Focus."

"Yes, you're right, although that is a tall order, considering. Are you still sure Keats is okay?"

Her next mumble was soft and sweetly reassuring. Keats never used a tone like that. He liked bossing me around, whereas Frost seemed to want to lead with love.

"You're very kind, Frost. I bet you'll make a great mom someday."

Her next mumble was the same as the first. "Focus."

Maternal. That's what it was. Whereas Keats was often an impatient taskmaster, she was soothing.

Not that I wanted to compare my dog to any other and find him wanting. He was exactly the dog I needed. However, it seemed his sister was pretty cool, too.

I touched her shoulder and energy flowed up my arm. It was warm, just as Keats' was, but more relaxing. In fact, I blinked a few times, thinking it might be nice to pull onto the shoulder and grab a quick nap.

Percy stepped into the breach with another nip, this time to my forearm. He wasn't about to let sweet maternal vibes derail our plan.

Such as it was.

For the moment, I had no plan, other than to drive along a road I'd only traveled once, on the way to Thistledown, and wait till I got my orders from prescient pets.

My phone rang in my front pocket. Pulling it out, I checked the screen. "Uh-oh. It's Kellan."

Percy meowed a suggestion to ignore it, and Frost mumbled the opposite. I figured she was probably right, the voice of reason. As long as these rings were on my finger—I checked and made sure they still were—I had a duty and obligation to take Kellan's calls no matter how annoyed he was at me.

Frost set a motherly paw on my knee to emphasize the lesson.

"Got it," I said and then pressed the button. "Hi, Kellan. How goes the search?"

"We'll find him, I promise." He sounded upbeat. Confident. Was it possible he didn't know what I was doing right now? If so, I'd best play along.

"I know you will. Thank you. Are you following the tracks of the ATV?"

"Yeah." He was outside and I heard voices in the background. "At least we were until the trail ended at a side road. One of the local cops went to get his hounds and they'll track him down in a jiffy."

Kellan had never, to my knowledge, used the word "jiffy" before. Jiffy wasn't a cop sort of word. Maybe he was just trying to buoy my spirits.

"What about George?" I asked. "Mr. Barrick's sheepdog knows the terrain well."

"He's with Edna's group, along with Maud, and Frost is with Gertie and Lou."

I noticed he gave leadership credit to our octogenarian warriors rather than the police. And also, that no one had realized Frost was missing yet. Maud and Lou must each have assumed she was with the other.

Glancing at the dog, I saw her mouth open in a pant-laugh that was very like her brother's, if less exuberant. Though proud of herself, she probably didn't like pulling the wool over her owner's eyes, even for a good cause.

"Sounds like it's well in hand," I said. "I'll check in as soon as the doctors give me the all-clear. Hopefully you'll have found Keats by then, though."

I fought to keep a quaver out of my voice and perhaps I was too successful, because there was a subtle shift in the energy coming down the line.

"So, you're on your way to the ER right now?"

Ugh. I couldn't lie to him. Even if I wanted to, Mama Frost's paw tapped my leg twice for no.

"That was your plan, right?" It wasn't a lie but an evasion. I glanced at Frost and got hit with a double shot of green-eyed disapproval.

"Yeah, I was worried about you, what with the bloody gash in your hair and all."

"Drying nicely," I said. That much was true. "I'm feeling fine right now."

"Even without food? You should be starving."

He was onto me, I suspected, but I kept going. "Who could eat at a time like this? My dog is missing."

"I bet you'd love a mint chocolate chip shake. Hold the chips."

Busted. So very busted.

I let out the breath I didn't realize I was holding. My voice probably sounded like I was high on helium. "Honestly? I wish I had that shake about now. Might settle my stomach. It's a bit queasy."

"Ivy. You are in over your head this time. Way over your head."

"Why? This thing is no harder to drive than the truck. Easier, actually."

"How about breaking the law by stealing a police vehicle? Was that easy, too?"

"Far from it. Getting in through the window was a squeeze with bruised ribs."

"Dodging the point. About breaking the law."

I waited a beat. "I didn't feel good about it, no. But I didn't want to leave and none of you were listening to me."

He gave an exasperated sigh. "That's because you were unconscious for the most part. When you did speak, it made no sense."

"I'm sure I made complete sense."

"Oh yeah? You asked for your mother. Twice."

"For my—? Are you sure you heard right?"

"There were witnesses. And if you, Ivy Galloway, are calling out for Dahlia, I have every reason to feel you should not be behind the wheel of any vehicle, let alone a police car."

"Obviously I was having a nightmare," I said. "But it's all good now."

"Do you know where you're going?"

"More or less." There was silence at his end and the dog tapped my leg again. "And Frost seems quite confident that Keats is alive and well. That's done more to lift my spirits than a mint shake, I must say."

"Frost is there? How did she—?" His grunt was even more

exasperated. "Percy is in cahoots with her, too. You should have seen his tragic portrayal of a bereaved cat on the hood of the police car. It distracted everyone and I guess she stowed away."

"She's quite clever, unsurprisingly. When I woke up she was hiding under Asher's coat in the rear footwell behind him."

"Clever indeed. And where is she taking you?"

"I honestly don't know. Can't understand her quite the way I do Keats. But she's riding shotgun with Percy and she'll let me know."

The next sigh held a hint of despair. "You're driving a cop car on the highway with a dog and cat in full view. There were burrs in your hair."

Patting the crown of my head, I felt a prickle. "Just a few. Anyway, we left the highway when you called. I have full confidence Frost will get me where I need to go."

"Our system tracks vehicles, you know. I guess I'll pull some officers off the search party to bring you in. You'll be subject to the laws of this region, by the way. I have no control over that."

Frost had turned away from me to poke the window with her nose. It was just as effective as a point. Maybe more so, although I'd never tell Keats that.

"Kellan, please don't call anyone off the hunt. I'll park the squad car soon and walk."

"That doesn't reassure me at all, Ivy. You've been injured and could get lost in the woods. It's cold out there."

"Frost won't let that happen. Will you, girl?"

Her yip had a warbling quality to it. The ring of confidence, I decided. Perhaps Kellan heard it that way, too, because I felt the tension between us ease slightly.

"If she's anything like her brother," he said, "I know she'll do her very best."

"Like they say in Hollywood, she's the same only different.

Much gentler than my boy, but with my hard-headedness I guess he needs to be persistent."

"Hmmmm." Kellan tactfully avoided agreeing with Keats, no doubt out of respect for my injuries. "The very second you know where Dalton Park is, you call me back, Ivy. This felon buried someone on my turf and I don't intend to let that happen again."

"You got it," I said, slowing even more as we drove into Thistledown proper.

The phone clicked, leaving an odd, heavy silence in the squad car. Percy's paws were on the dashboard and Frost's head was out the window. The dog took in deep gusts, ran them over her brilliant sheepdog neurons, and then finally passed a verdict. It came by way of her tail, which bristled suddenly. A growl drifted back to me that was higher than Keats' but no less chilling. Percy, who'd apparently accepted her fully as the substitute Keats, added a hiss for good measure.

We were close to where we needed to be, obviously, although I couldn't imagine why Dalton would choose to hide out with my pilfered dog near the main drag in town. Why hadn't he stolen a proper vehicle and run when he had the chance? Or at least found a good place to go to ground? Wendel's wouldn't be the only bunker around.

"Well, that's strange," I said. "The light's on in the library and it's after nine p.m. Maybe Thelma worries about break-ins and leaves it lit."

Frost's tail stayed stiff and straight, as if Thelma was right to worry.

"I suppose she might work late, but is library business really that pressing around here? Especially for a woman in her eighties?"

As we passed, I took my foot off the gas to coast. The image of a shark flashed through my mind. Now, I wasn't a corporate shark but a land shark in a squad car. How times had changed.

"Do you see that? Someone's pacing in the schoolhouse, and it isn't Thelma. Strides are long, like a man's. Janitor, maybe?" I slowed even more and practically pressed my nose to the driver's window. "Okay. Not a janitor. I'm afraid there's trouble in the stacks, you two. Good thing I love sorting a library out."

CHAPTER THIRTY-ONE

Thistledown Public Library was the last place I expected to find a killer, which probably made it a good place to hide.

Dalton Park wasn't keeping a low profile, however. If I could see him from the road, others could, too. He seemed agitated and I wondered if that meant Keats had escaped. His colleagues sounded ruthless, so he probably didn't want to leave town empty-handed.

Frost and Percy lashed their tails in unison, ready for our next act. I was, too, but I hoped Thelma was long gone. A shootout would very likely ruffle even the stiffest curls.

Now, all I needed was a gun.

Or preferably hired guns.

Grabbing my phone, I tapped a short message to Kellan, Edna, Gertie, and Wendel Barrick. I had no idea who was closest at the moment, but someone well-armed would arrive soon. In the meantime, we'd get the lay of the library, as it were.

I let the police car ease past. Dalton's restless pacing continued and it seemed unlikely that he'd noticed us. The last thing I needed was for him to make any impulsive moves.

Frost offered a gentle mumble that nearly made me smile. It sounded like she was suggesting the last thing I needed was to make any impulsive moves myself.

If Keats were here, he'd be threatening all kinds of impulsive moves. I appreciated Frost keeping a level head when my world had never felt quite so topsy-turvy.

"Can't promise anything," I said. "But if Keats and Thelma are safe and Dalton stays put, we'll wait for reinforcements. This guy already outmaneuvered me tonight and my ego's still smarting."

Frost's next mumble was reassuring. A "he'll regret it" sort of message. I liked the sound of that. Dalton's place was in the slammer, not the library. Preferably with scars to keep the memory of this night perpetually alive.

I pulled the squad car into the bushes on the quiet side street, turned off the engine and looked around for a weapon. All I had on me was my utility knife, which wouldn't hold up well against a sociopath.

We got out, and I opened the back door to check the footwell, too.

Bingo! Asher's hockey stick. It wasn't a graceful weapon but it was better than nothing.

Propping it over my shoulder, I closed the door, locked the car and pocketed the key. The pets led me on a short path through the bushes till we were close to the old schoolhouse. Percy ran ahead to leap onto a wooden bin at the side of the building that probably held trash cans or garden tools. Setting the hockey stick on the ground, I sat on the bin, swung my legs around and rose on my knees beside the cat. Frost joined us and we stared inside.

The scene unfolding was like a very strange play indeed. A drama in an unlikely setting with even less likely characters.

Dalton Park was the obvious villain, pacing across the open

space in front of the checkout desk. He had looked princely at our first encounter, but scratches and dried blood from Percy's interventions had left him looking like a zombie out of Edna's apocalypse.

Percy couldn't help giving a purr of pride but I silenced him with a squeeze. There would be time to bask later, after we'd rescued Thelma from her "cockpit." Waiting for reinforcements was out of the question now.

The elderly librarian was sitting on her usual stool, looking utterly composed. Her hands were folded neatly on the desk and it took me a second to notice they were bound with white rope.

She was still wearing her black mourning suit, and her lap under the desk appeared to be covered with a crocheted blanket.

A blanket that looked oddly familiar.

It was Dalton's net, I realized—the one that had trapped us earlier, judging by the rips and tears.

As I stared, an eerie blue glint caught my eye. I felt a rumble in my chest as my heart lurched back to life.

Keats was lying on Thelma's lap and trying to tell me something. Pulling out my phone, I took a photo without the flash, and blew it up so I could see more detail.

While Dalton paced and Thelma covered for the dog, Keats had chewed through the net. At this point, he was free to go, but he was waiting for the right moment.

Waiting for me, probably. He trusted I would come.

I pressed my palm to the window lightly and sent him a silent message to hold on just a bit longer.

Frost jumped down and led us around the schoolhouse to the back. Underneath an open window stood an old barrel that looked ready to split. If it had held Dalton, however, it could hold me.

It took some dexterity to wriggle onto it without tipping but soon I was looking into what appeared to be a storage room. The glass was open and the screen slit, so clearly that had been the killer's point of entry with my netted dog.

Frost had moved away to stand under another window, where the light was on. Percy seemed to endorse her opinion that it was the better choice.

Reluctantly, I jumped off, tipped the barrel and rolled it into position. Any movement at all caused sharp bolts of pain from my ribs but I didn't have the luxury of pampering them. In fact, I took a moment now to swallow a couple of painkillers from the stash I kept in my bib pocket for migraines. It was worth the delay if it kept me mobile.

Standing the barrel up again, I climbed aboard and found myself peering into Thelma's office. A large map under glass covered her desk and a scroll of some type lay half-unfurled on top.

I went to work on the old wooden frame with my fingernails. Luckily, the latch had long since rusted out and the window rose with a creaky groan. I stopped and waited, and when it seemed safe, began lifting again. When there was enough access, I pulled out my knife and cut the screen.

Getting through this window quietly with injured ribs wasn't going to be easy, but I had no choice. Behind me, Frost touched my calf gently. With Keats, it would have been a sharp nip that left holes in my overalls.

Her signal worked as well as a bite and I got moving. It was no worse than breaking into the cop car. Except for the fact there was a man inside with a gun and my most treasured possession.

I maneuvered the hockey stick through the window first and rested it carefully against the wall. Then I hoisted myself over the frame until I could slide onto the floor inside. Percy followed with an elegant leap. He landed on Thelma's desk, where he started scraping invisible litter over the unfurled chart. I hoped the only passing Percy predicted was Dalton's but there was no time to find out. Turning, I lifted Frost through the window to prevent scrabbling claws from alerting our hosts to the intrusion. Then I chased the first two painkillers with a couple more and hoped they'd kick in fast.

Peeking out the door into the long hall, I saw a couple of carts full of books lined up against the wall. One was within easy reach, so I hooked it with an index finger and pulled it toward me.

The cart became my portable shield. Kneeling, I signaled Frost to get into line behind me. She dropped to her belly, just as she was wired to do in pursuit of sheep. Meanwhile, Percy jumped onto the middle shelf of the cart and stared through the books.

After covering a couple of yards I realized my progress was too slow. Too choppy. Too obvious. Things would go better if I copied Frost.

I dropped to the worn carpet and crawled, belly down, nudging the cart ahead of me and dragging the hockey stick along. Doing the army crawl with bruised ribs should gain me a promotion in Edna's militia, I figured.

If I survived.

If we all survived.

Why hadn't help arrived by now?

That reminded me to silence my phone. I would hate for a cheery ping to ruin a remarkable ambush.

My concern proved unnecessary, however, as my phone had finally died. Whatever happened now, I was on my own. Except for an audacious cat and the second-best dog in the world. A good team. A very good team. And the painkillers were finally kicking in.

Still, it took ages to pull myself down the hall inch by inch, behind the cart.

At least we could eavesdrop on the conversation, and what I heard surprised me. Dalton seemed to have lost his Terminator cool. He was rambling, both physically and verbally, while Thelma responded with the poise of a trained FBI negotiator.

"Young man, I'm quite sure you can find your way out of Thistledown tonight. There aren't enough police in the region to block every avenue. Have you considered Crow's Lane?"

"Crow's might work," he said. "What else?"

"Stenway Road is good this time of night. I gave up my license a year ago or I'd drive you myself."

He turned to stare at her. "Why are you being so nice? You were never nice to me when I lived here. We called you the Schoolhouse Witch."

Thelma smiled. It was the first time I'd seen her teeth. "Oh, I know you kids called me that but my motives were always good. I was trying to instill a love of learning the education system of the day failed to do. So many of your era had great potential. You and Sunny Bibb, in particular. I could see a spark in your eyes. Of course, all you wanted to do was roughhouse in my stacks. I'm sorry I cracked down too hard and caused the opposite reaction."

His eyes looked a little dazed. "Not really. There was a reason we hung out here. I suppose we knew on some level you were trying to help."

"Things at home were difficult for some children in our region," Thelma said. "I tried to do my bit with story hour, book club and craft day, but I was no match for the prevailing culture."

"A culture of abuse." Dalton started pacing again. "Half of us were beaten senseless on the regular."

Thelma nodded and I noticed one of her rigid curls had

flipped. It was the only outward sign she was flustered. "I'm working with a colleague to map out a family tree for the entire region, you know. That's why I was here so late tonight. Your family is on it."

"A family of no-good losers," he said. "Like me."

"Never too late to turn over a new leaf. You can start by borrowing a car and escaping town by one of the routes I suggested. Leave the three of us in peace."

Three? As far as I knew she wasn't aware I was there yet, and she wouldn't likely give me away if she did.

There must be someone else in the library.

A muffled grumble gave me an idea where to look. Angling the book cart, I saw a gagged woman seated on the floor and roped to the nonfiction section. It was appropriate for a journalist, or at least someone who claimed that title.

Justine Schalow had once again managed to be in the wrong place at the right time for a story.

My ribs hadn't made me groan but the sight of Justine nearly did. There was fear in her eyes but worse, defiance. Given the opportunity, she would make this mission difficult, if not scuttle it completely.

"Where would I borrow a car, Miss Tilrow?" Dalton asked. "You gave yours up, I suppose?"

"I'm afraid so, but a man of your skills could probably get a parked car going, no?"

"Maybe, but thanks to that stupid cat, just the sight of me on the street will have people calling the cops."

"Oh Dalton, you'll be fine. Pull your hood up and work quickly. Leave the dog here so your hands are free. We're not going anywhere. Your rope has seen to that."

"I guess. You're always a lady, Miss T. It's the other one I worry about." He moved to Justine and tightened her restraints.

"Good thing I found her outside. I think she was planning to break in."

"It's a popular place tonight," Thelma said. "I'm relieved you gagged her."

"Yeah. She talks twice as much as Ivy Galloway."

"And how is Ivy?" Thelma asked. "My colleague in Clover Grove is fond of her."

He scuffed the carpet with one boot. "She fell into a bunker and I left her there. Sorry, Miss T."

"You did what you had to do, I suppose, and Ivy will likely be fine. Perhaps you could send me the details once you've cleared town. There's no time for it now."

He nodded and paced.

Paced and nodded.

It seemed like Dalton was as stuck as I was right now.

Thelma happened to glance around at that moment, and saw the cart had moved. There wasn't a stick of furniture in the place that she hadn't mentally catalogued, I was sure. Her eyes seemed to drill through the books as she put the pieces together. Then she gave a little nod.

Turning back to her captor, she started again. "I don't want to alarm you, Dalton, but I saw a police cruiser drive by. I'm sure it was just routine, but perhaps you should take a quick look down the road and confirm before you do anything more."

Her smile was even sweeter than her tone, and little surprised me more than those tools being part of her repertoire.

"Will do," Dalton said, unlocking the front door. "Hang tight, Miss T."

I hoped our troops were standing by outside but couldn't lie around waiting to find out. Instead, I whispered to Percy and Frost to stay. Then I pushed myself up to a stooped crouch and ran to Thelma's desk. My fingers touched Keats for the briefest second, and I pulled in every bit of warmth from his brown eye before slicing the rope tying Thelma's hands.

"The door, Ivy," she said. "Lock the door."

It was already too late. Hearing boots on the ramp, I retreated, whispering, "On my signal, Thelma. Romantic poets for the win."

I rushed back to my cart and hit the floor a little too hard. Adrenaline kept most of the pain at bay, but I felt that collision.

Dalton pulled the door open and came inside. "Miss T, I always hated your sharp eyes but this time you're a genius. The cop car is in the bush and the passenger window is open. I can throw the dog in ahead of me and then hot-wire it. Perfect way to blow this town."

My queasy stomach roiled harder. The ploy that had worked *for* me was now going to work against me. Why hadn't I thought to roll up the window?

"You'd better hurry before the officer comes back," she said. "I suggest leaving the dog behind. Animals are too unpredictable. Why not take me as a hostage? A librarian is always an asset."

He stared at her, looking for a hitch, but her smile held steady. If he'd been more observant, perhaps he would have noticed that her rogue curl had flipped back into place. That was her first priority with free hands. Now her fingers were laced again, with the rope arranged overtop.

"I wish I could, Miss T. Guess I knew you were an ally, which is why I came here tonight when the ATV broke down." He shook his head sadly. "The dog's the one with value to my colleagues. I was supposed to get Farmer Galloway but I can't go back completely empty-handed."

"Hold the longer view, Dalton. I've been following the rise of crime in hill country and I think there's a way to play this. Especially for a young man with your abilities."

His eyes glazed just for a second, as if fighting the seductive power of her belief in him. I hated feeling even a twinge of empathy for this man but it was impossible not to, after hearing his story.

That said, I would do my best to take him down before he could take anyone else down. He was just a heartbeat away from realizing he should kill Thelma and Justine for knowing too much.

"Thank you, ma'am," he said, "but I need to take the dog."

"Very well, then. Perhaps it's for the best as he's made a mess of my mourning suit."

As Dalton walked over to the desk, both the librarian and Keats glanced at me. I raised my hand in a pistol and pretended to shoot. Go time.

In the precise moment that Thelma pushed her stool back, Keats exploded from her lap into Dalton's face. The dog's snarl was more menacing than I'd ever heard it.

Careening backward, Dalton somehow managed to pull his gun from his pocket. Before he could take aim, Thelma jumped to her feet, grabbed another cart of books, and swung it around with impressive force and accuracy. She drove the end into Dalton's midriff so hard that he dropped the gun. Then she plowed him into the aisle with the romantic poets.

I was right behind her with my cart. Once he was well back in the stacks, I blocked him there.

The romantic poets couldn't hold a man like Dalton for long, however. He roared a string of words Thelma would normally never permit in her establishment and hurled a couple of heavy books at us.

"Stop that right now," she said, kicking the gun aside with a sensible Oxford. "Show some respect for our greatest writers, if not yourself."

"Stuff it, you old witch. I was right about you all along and now you're going to pay."

He put one boot on a shelf and started to climb. When he looked up, however, a fluffy orange assailant leaned over and hissed a blatant taunt.

"Not again," Dalton said. "This time, I'll wring your neck, cat."

He backed down, though, and decided to go through the shelves instead. There was hardly enough clearance but he bashed at the metal and bent it, and then forced his upper body through the gap.

I was waiting on the other side with Dickens, the Brontë sisters and other warriors of Victorian fiction.

Not to mention my brother's hockey stick, as well as two dogs working in tandem. Any sibling rivalry between Keats and Frost fell by the wayside as they cornered their quarry.

"Dude, I'd stay where you are," I said. "One slapshot to the head and you're done."

His inner Terminator rose again and he started thrashing through the gap in the books, grunting staccato threats. "I. Will. Kill. You." More books fell to the floor. "First the cat. Then the dogs. Then the witch. Then you."

"What about the reporter?" I said, angling the hockey stick. It would be hard to get a good swing. "Surely she should go first."

"Excuse me?" The voice was Justine's, so Thelma must have set her free. "This is no time for jokes, Ivy."

Dalton hurled a book at me, which struck my arm and fell to the floor.

"You'd better not hit Keats with Keats," I said. "Justine, do you know how to fire a gun?"

"I'll give it a go," she said. "Head or butt?"

"Never mind," Thelma said. "You'll hurt one of the pets.

Luckily, I'm an excellent markswoman, and it would give me no greater pleasure than to erase this fellow from my hill country criminal family tree."

"I'm a great shot, too," a man called. "For my age or any age."

It was Wendel Barrick and I had no doubt he was telling the truth.

"Me too," another man said. It was Rickie Merriweather. "And so's my wife. Good thing you had plenty of firearms, Wendel."

"Always like to overprepare," Mr. Barrick said.

"I've never fired a gun," Louisa Gentry said. "But since he stole our dog, maybe I could have first dibs."

Wendel shrugged. "Ladies first, then. You and Thelma flip a coin."

In the end, another lady took the honors. Frost gave Dalton's wrist a rather savage nip, judging by his yell.

Keats cast his sister a look of disgust and mumbled something like, "I'll show you how it's done."

Standing on his rear legs like a circus dog, he danced easily away from Dalton's swinging fists and then clamped his fangs into the man's earlobe.

The scream was immensely gratifying and soon doubled, as Frost followed her brother's lead. After all, there was an ear for each of them.

George was trying to get in on the action and there was a nose available. Wendel called him off, however. "Hold up, sheepdog militia. I'm going to shoot off one digit at a time till this deadbeat spits out who he's working for. We need to put this sorry business to bed."

"I've got that covered, Mr. Barrick," Kellan said, as uniformed officers crowded into the schoolhouse library with the rest of my friends. "Back off, everyone."

"I want to know who was targeting the dogs and me," I said, as the police moved in with the romantic poets and yanked Dalton out from behind. "Let Wendel shoot off his piggies till he goes wee wee wee all the way home."

Thelma pulled me aside. "There's no need for more blood-shed in my establishment, thank you very much. The special project that keeps me here late at night might very well give you and the authorities the answers you need."

"I'm banking on it," Justine said, waving her phone as she came out of Thelma's office. "Thanks for the head start, Miss T."

Kellan grabbed the phone from Justine's hand as she passed and she lashed out at him. "That's my property, Chief. You can't just—"

My brother caught her hand, twisted her around and then perp-walked her to the door. She was only a few feet behind Dalton, now cuffed, and put up nearly as good a fight.

"I'll put this one away for safekeeping," Asher called. "Luckily someone ditched my car nearby."

Hearing that, my umbrage subsided rather quickly and I let Jilly lead me to a quiet corner and ease me to the floor. "I'd rather be in the stacks," I said. "Everyone's staring."

She passed me a pack of tissues. "That's because you're filthy."

"And crying like a baby," Edna said, joining us with Gertie. "What kind of behavior is that for a soldier?"

"Oh, give me a break, Edna. I've had a bit of a day."

Keats curled up in my lap, mumbling a detailed account of all that I'd missed. I pulled off his coat so he could get comfort-able and he nudged it aside with obvious contempt. He prob-ably blamed everything on that jacket. I was glad to see his abduction hadn't changed the essentials, because there wasn't a single cell in this dog's body I didn't adore.

An unexpected defender took up my cause. "Miss Evans," Thelma said, "Ivy army-crawled down that long hall shielded only by a book cart. An impressive maneuver."

"You belly crawled with bruised ribs?" Edna asked me.

"Cracked, I'm sure," I said. "Hurt like stink."

Thelma gave Edna a pucker. "This young lady saved my life and is a soldier in every sense of the word."

Edna looked somewhat chastened, either because Thelma was a couple of years her senior or because her curls out-curled Edna's perm. "If Ivy saved your life, I suppose we can tolerate some bragging."

"Thelma's the true hero," I said. "She offered herself as a hostage in exchange for Keats." I stared up at the librarian, hugging my dog close. "I can never thank you enough for that."

"We share a love of Keats, the poet. That's all I needed to know to do my very best for you and this dog." She glanced at Edna and gave her a wink. "At our age, we can afford to take a few risks."

Edna and Gertie both winked back. It was like witnessing the secret handshake of the octogenarian warrior.

"Did you really give up your license?" I asked Thelma.

"Of course not. I've got a brand new Range Rover sitting in my driveway. Do you think I'd ever let that rabble behind the wheel?"

"So, all your talk about him being a troubled hill country youth was a lie?" I asked.

She patted her curls to make sure they were locked down. "Not at all. But everyone has a chance to make better choices as an adult. Instead, he decided to bury a man equally troubled and half as blessed in the brains department."

Jilly sat down beside me, and I saw Asher coming our way. My best friend was probably creating a human shield from a very angry brother.

"I'm sorry," I blurted, before he could say anything. "Everyone was right about my needing medical treatment. I didn't know what I was doing."

"Not buying it, twisty sis," he said. "When I saw your butt disappearing into my squad car, the first thing I thought was... she's got moves. And the second thing I thought was... she really does need more food if she fits through there. So I borrowed thermal bags from Buck Burgers and brought dinner along." He handed me a huge cup, beaded with moisture. "Enjoy your mint chocolate chip shake. Hold the chips."

I wanted to cry again but Frost nudged the cup and I took a sip instead. After thanking my brother, I caught Maud Gentry's eye. "She's sweet," I said, over a rumble of protest from my own dog. "And fierce."

"Very," Thelma agreed. "She'll make a good mother."

Maud smiled as her dog returned to her side. "One day."

Thelma tipped her head coyly. "More like sixty-two. Normal gestation after yesterday's liaison."

"She didn't," Maud said, sounding horrified. "Who?"

"Promise you'll return E.B. White's essays tomorrow and I'll tell you." Thelma waited till Maud nodded and then gestured across the library. "There's your Casanova."

"George?" Maud said. "He has to be fifteen years old."

I raised my cup to George and then Frost. "He's thirteen. And a prizewinner of great heart. I'd say Frost chose well because champion sheepdogs will never lack homes."

Maud sighed. "She could have done worse, I suppose. But the problem of keeping these dogs safe remains."

"We'll have a summit," Jilly said, as Percy climbed down onto her shoulder. "You're all invited to Runaway Inn for Thanksgiving. We have so much to be thankful for, don't we?"

"Puppies, Uncle Keats," I said, hugging him even tighter. "Christmas comes in January this year."

CHAPTER THIRTY-TWO

"It'll be fine," Kellan said, squeezing my hand. "Everything's going to be fine."

"You can't know that," I said.

"I do, though. I feel good about this decision. Very good."

I curled the fingers of my free hand into Keats' fur as he stretched out on my lap. With the temperature above freezing, the winter jacket hadn't been a bone of contention today. It was a relief. After what happened last night, I couldn't bear the idea of arguing with my wonderful dog ever again.

Keats mumbled cheerfully, probably planning how to exploit my guilt and anxiety for his personal gain. There would be no coats, no ponds and most certainly no baths.

"You'll stink," I said. "How do you feel about that?"

"Pardon me?" Kellan sounded horrified.

I stared at him and then laughed. "Not you. Keats. We're future planning."

He shook his head. "Isn't that what *we're* doing? I stepped away from a crime scene for that very purpose and I can assure you I showered this morning. Unlike your other companion."

"I know, and I'm sorry, Kellan. I'm just a little preoccupied with what went down yesterday."

He squeezed my hand again. "It's barely been 12 hours since you and the stinker were attacked. The doctor said it would take time to recover, remember? Take it easy, she said."

I remembered, but I actually felt pretty good and hadn't argued when Kellan stopped at the jeweler Thelma Tilrow recommended. We had bigger things to worry about than big rings, but Kellan had been determined to get this done. Maybe he wanted to check something off his long to-do list. Or maybe he felt a little superstitious, too. Last night we had come close to being very unlucky indeed.

The jeweler had given us some privacy while Kellan talked me into letting him remove the rubber washer and then the diamond. The agreement was that we'd do one ring at a time.

"Do you feel any different right now?" I asked, pulling my hand away and checking the status of my garnets. I felt a little naked with only one ring, and a loose one at that.

"About a lot of things, yes. About marrying you, no."

Tension seeped out of me with his reassurance. I had worried stealing Asher's squad car might be one step too far.

"I'm sorry about escaping custody," I said. "I know it made you look bad in front of your Thistledown colleagues."

"You were never in custody, Ivy. Your brother was just driving you to the ER. That said, your devious moves point to gaps in our protocols. I can probably make a case to the township for upgrading some of our squad cars."

"Twisty," I said. "That's Asher's word and I like it better than devious."

I could tell he wanted to say more but the nature of our current mission probably stopped him. Maybe, like me, he wanted us to have a perpetual clean slate in case something happened. I vowed not to exploit his goodwill, unlike a certain sheepdog.

Keats mumbled something that sounded like, "You do you."

"Glad he's none the worse for that misadventure," Kellan said. "I can't tell you much about my chat with Dalton Park, but I got some good information out of him."

Even more tension seeped away. "Really? How'd you make him talk?"

"Thelma Tilrow shared an exhaustive list of potential contacts and our database produced some immediate hits. My counterparts in Dorset Hills have two people in custody already. That loosened his tongue."

"So Dalton's gangster colleagues won't be coming after us? I wouldn't put it past them to steal Frost and old George to build a breeding program. Their very own sheepdog militia."

"I feel pretty good about that, too," he said, grabbing my hand again and squeezing. "But don't take it from me. What does Officer Keats think?"

Keats stared at Kellan with his blue eye and then let me know with his brown one that all was well. For now, anyway. Still, he gave a little whine that made me ask, "Any clues about Anne's whereabouts? One of those goons must have her."

Kellan gave a single shake of his head. "Not yet. But we'll keep looking. So don't *you* go looking. Please?"

I gave a single shake of my head, too. One shake was non-committal in my books. For the moment, I wasn't fit to search for Anne myself, but if the police came up empty, I'd have no choice. This was Keats' mother, after all. The spectacular dog who produced mine, and then Frost.

But that was a problem better tackled down the road. Today was about recovery and celebration.

"Thelma will be thrilled about the arrests," I said. "She's in a competition with Dottie Bridges and this will put her far in the lead."

He laughed. "I had no idea the library business was so cutthroat."

"And I had no idea there were so many strong women of a certain age. Feels great knowing they have my back."

His fingers relaxed. "I'd like to think I can protect you. That's what I've pledged to do. Obviously, there's room for improvement."

Now it was my turn to squeeze. "What happened was my fault. I knew better than to go into that barn on my own and I even thought twice about it. Curiosity got the better of me. Again." A shudder ran over Keats from ears to tail. "This was a lesson I won't forget or conveniently ignore. The deadbeats hit me where I live this time."

The jeweler came out and offered the diamond ring on a red velvet tray. It sparkled more than I remembered. Maybe everything just looked brighter today after a crisis.

"It's time," Kellan said, releasing my hand and taking the diamond off the tray. "Cough up the garnets."

My fingers balled into a fist. "Can't we just stick the diamond ring on top? Since it's been downsized, I won't need the rubber washer anymore."

"You're worrying about nothing."

"I'm worrying about jinxing our engagement." I looked up at the jeweler. "Tell him I'm not alone."

"You're not alone," he said, giving me a fatherly smile. More like grandfatherly, given the shock of white hair. "But I'll get your other ring done in a jiffy."

"A jiffy?" I turned to Kellan. "You used that word last night."

"Jiffy? It doesn't sound like me."

"Exactly. Strange things happen sometimes. Inexplicable things."

He shrugged. "Ivy, I will meet you at the altar no matter what strange words slip out of my mouth under pressure." He tried prying my fingers open and then looked up at the jeweler. "Help a guy, will you?"

The jeweler's grin showed under a bristly white moustache. "A lot of people feel the same way about that old superstition. But I've sized a lot of rings in my career and never lost a single fiancé over it. You can trust me, young lady."

I didn't trust him or anyone else outside my immediate circle right now. It was too soon.

Keats gave a mumble of frustration and jumped down. The time for sitting with our feelings had apparently passed. A busy sheepdog was a happy sheepdog.

Once he had four on the floor, he sank 42 teeth in my calf. Or at least enough of them to hurt.

"Stop that! You know nothing about superstition."

My dog knew plenty about motivation and opened wide to deliver another dose of it.

I jumped up and moved away from him. "Your sister is so sweet. Maybe I'll trade you in for a nicer model once those pups arrive."

A strategic dive made me jump and the garnet ring flew off my finger and rolled to the counter. Keats nabbed it and trotted over to the jeweler. The man held out the tray and the dog dropped the slobbery garnets onto the velvet.

"Well, that's a first," the jeweler said, heading through a curtain into the back room. "Thelma sends me the most interesting referrals."

I flicked my hand at Keats. "The least you could do is watch him work. Make sure there's no switcheroo back there. Those garnets belonged to Kellan's mother."

The dog trotted over and stuck his head through the curtain. He kept looking back at me, letting me know I wasn't the only one feeling sentimental today. We'd nearly lost each other and it would take time—and perhaps more arrests among Dalton's colleagues—to feel comfortable being apart.

"Are you going to make me go down on one knee again?" Kellan asked, holding the diamond ring between his index finger and thumb.

"Not for fifty years," I said. "We'll do one of those recommitment things then."

He slipped the ring on my finger and grinned. "If I can still kneel, you've got a deal."

It wasn't long at all until the garnets were back on my finger. As we left, I offered Kellan my right hand.

"I know what you're doing," he said. "Twisty miss."

My left hand was tucked deep into the side pocket of my overalls. "What? I'm just keeping the dust off my gemstones."

"You're putting that rubber washer back on, when it's been rendered completely unnecessary."

"I like it," I said. "It's the latest in farmer fashion."

He shook his head. "The first of many adjustments I'll need to make, I suppose."

"Probably. I'll evict Mom before the big day. She'll be ready by then."

"No need. While I don't exactly relish a daily dose of Dahlia, marriage is all about compromise."

We walked down the sidewalk and he opened the door of his squad car for me. The front door, happily. One day a common criminal, the next Cinderella.

"Mom's been driving Jilly and Asher nuts. The inn's big, but maybe not big enough for five of us."

"Let's just see how things go," he said.

That's what he always said when he was trying to avoid a touchy topic. "What does that mean?"

He tried to close the door while I propped it open. "Can't we just enjoy the day after near-disaster?"

I pulled my hand out of my pocket and stared at the three rings. "I knew I shouldn't have parted with them. Now you're keeping secrets from me."

He shut the door, walked around the car and got behind the wheel. Turning the key in the ignition, he turned to me. "Asher is gunning for a promotion and there's more opportunity in other jurisdictions. It could mean some change for our best friends."

Not so long ago, the very thought of Jilly moving away rattled me to the core. But that was before Kellan proposed. I knew when I accepted these beautiful rings that it would mean change. He was going to give up his own place to share mine with more than 60 animals, rotating guests, and possibly my mother. My sisters were in and out all the time and my dad frequently slept in the barn.

Obviously, I'd need to compromise, too.

I pulled off the rubber washer and handed it to him in a show of faith. No risk, no reward.

He slipped it into his uniform pocket with a grin. "Jilly and Asher will never go far. We need them too much."

Settling back into the seat, I scratched Keats' ears. For once, my dog and I were at peace. "Asher isn't the only one looking forward to a promotion," I said. "Soon, I'll be the Twisty Missus."

CHAPTER THIRTY-THREE

Jilly called from the porch and I jumped down from the manure pile. Thanksgiving dinner was about to be served and I'd evaded the real work long enough. It was funny how turning manure felt like blissful respite whereas hosting felt like hard labor.

That said, this was a banner holiday with plenty of friends old and new. There were tables set up all over the main floor to accommodate everyone, with beautiful decorations and place cards that left nothing to chance. Jilly knew the critical importance of putting the right people together.

But as I walked in, the wrong people were in the dining room, it seemed. I followed raised voices and found Thelma Tilrow and Dottie Bridges in a heated argument. My miniature ceramic Christmas village was already set up on the sideboard and Dottie was trying to wrestle a figurine out of her colleague's hand.

"What's going on?" I asked, holding out my hand, palm up. "My librarians have turned on each other."

Thelma reluctantly dropped a tiny elf into my hand. "This

little fellow was tipped over and I was trying to put him back in Santa's village."

"But the village is in the wrong place," Dottie said. "If this were to scale, he would be off the map."

"The north pole is definitely out of dining room range," I said, placing the elf back with Santa and his crew on the outskirts of my little town. "We do the best we can with the space we have."

Percy jumped lightly into the ceramic town and ignored Thelma when she tried to shoo him. Catching my eye, he swatted the elf onto its side. Turned out the first spill probably hadn't been an accident.

"Uh-oh," Jilly said, coming in with more cutlery. "What is my cat baby doing?"

"Nothing," I said, as Percy swung his paw back to scrape at the artificial snow. There was no need to tell these good women that Christmas wouldn't be Christmas without a murder. "Just provoking our guests."

"I don't know how you stand it, Ivy," Thelma said. Her silver curls were bigger today, but no less stiff. She clearly had another roller set for festive occasions. "This place is a zoo."

Twin prim puckers may have daunted someone else but I knew these ladies were fond of me. What's more, they were delighted about having direct access to the chief of police. The way they eyed Kellan when he came into the room told me there was more intel to share about hill country crime. The librarians were eager to help him trace the identities of the two older bodies from the gangster graveyard, and I was glad to yield the floor for a change.

It wasn't often I needed recovery time, but after what happened in Thistledown, I wanted to do nothing more than wander the farm and dance with my alpaca. My grandparents had arrived at noon with Bocelli the caroling donkey and Clippers the miniature horse, so I expected there would be more entertainment to follow. With any luck, Albert would join me.

Keats hadn't complained about boredom yet, but I predicted it would start after the last guest left.

For the moment, he was happy hosting his fellow sheepdogs, George and Frost. Hosting apparently meant ambushing his sister at every opportunity. She didn't give him many. No matter how twisty he was—and devious really did apply here—Frost saw or sensed him coming. It was all the more proof she'd be a good mom. Jilly and I were planning weekly visits to Thistledown after the happy day arrived. I wondered if my friend would be able to resist bringing a pup home with her.

Weekly visits would mean more time with Maud. I planned to learn all I could from her about animal management and training. She was working now with June Lunde's sheepdog and I was glad Skip would have a chance to discover what truly motivated him. The friendship between the breeders was growing, which would also give Louisa a little more freedom. In fact, Lou had gone on a hike with Zoe Hampton and learned that Sunny Bibb reached out after Dalton's abrupt departure from her life. I suspected the two old friends would heal the rift but the trust between Darnese and Maud was likely in terminal condition. What happened with Kale was shocking, but Darnese's lies nearly cost Maud another dearly loved dog. I believed in forgiveness, but that would likely be beyond my capacity, too.

Lou came over as soon as we all walked into the living room. Wendel Barrick was there chatting with Edna, Gertie and the Merriweathers.

"Did Thelma tell you she hired me, Ivy?" Lou asked. "And that she's going to teach me to shoot?"

Maud tuned into the conversation. "Shoot? How about you stick to filing books?"

"A young lady needs varied skills these days," Thelma said. "But her main responsibility will be keeping E.B. White's essays where they belong."

"Easy," Maud said, grinning. "Because they belong on my nightstand."

"We'll see about that," Thelma said. "Lou is also responsible for the library naughty list."

Wendel joined us. "Glad I'm in good standing. I'll have more time for reading now that I've done some hiring of my own. The Merriweathers have kindly agreed to manage my country estate at a very reasonable rate. What's more, they've agreed to live there and keep out the riffraff."

"It's nice not to *be* the riffraff," Rickie said, winking at me.

He and Madge were in matching sweaters and new jeans. It was wonderful to see them looking so content.

"You'll excuse me if I never step foot in that barn again," I said. "Or the bunker, for that matter."

"You're missing out on a fine piece of subterranean real estate," Edna said. "Never saw a better setup. Can't wait to take Buckley Brackens over for a look."

Madge grabbed Rickie's hand and beamed at me. "Your visit changed everything for us, Ivy. Feels good to have a real roof over our heads again."

"Still on our terms," Rickie said. "We'll work hard for the privilege."

"We've found our people," Madge said. "A small community but a good one."

I gestured around the packed room. "Not that small. Look at this community."

"Like the rings of Saturn," Jilly whispered behind me as she circulated with punch.

"What's that, Jillian?" Edna asked. "Has the chef been into the punch?"

More raised voices drifted downstairs. Mom and Asher were arguing over the bathroom again. Their bickering had diminished but both seemed to enjoy a bit of combat.

"Would you mind, Keats?" I asked. "So that the chef doesn't need to throw any punches?"

"Family," Kellan said. "What can you do?"

He dropped his left arm over my shoulder and I laughed out loud. On his ring finger was the rubber washer. It was a beautiful promise of a life filled with merriment.

Keats and Frost raced upstairs together. With a common goal, *his* family united instantaneously. Two sharp squeals followed.

"Might be blood," I said. "Good thing Mom's wearing scarlet."

"Are you sure you want to join the Galloway clan, Kellan?" Jilly asked.

He waggled the rubber washer at her. "Quite sure. One thing I'm incredibly happy to share is those sheepdog herding nips."

Asher jogged into the room ahead of Keats, while Mom followed with Frost. "Ivy, call this one off," she said. "You owe me ten dollars for the hose."

"Not my dog," I said. "And I owe Frost way more than ten bucks for service under pressure."

The room grew strangely silent and I sensed everyone pulling in a collective breath.

"What?" Kellan said. "Why is everyone staring— oof!"

Orange fluff landed on his shoulder suddenly and with a flourish. The dogs might spread themselves around, but Percy would always keep the chief on his toes.

I grabbed Kellan's left hand and squeezed. "Sorry. We'll grow on you. I promise."

He waited till the cat settled then leaned down to kiss my cheek. "No need for apologies. Our family is purrrr-fect just as it is."

Looking for Bought-the-Farm bonus content? Join the Ellen Riggs newsletter at **ellenrigss.com** for behind-the-scenes fun!

RUNAWAY FARM & INN RECIPES

Criminally Delicious Coconut Cream Pie

Ingredients

Baked 9-inch single-crust pastry shell
1/3 cup all purpose flour
2/3 cup sugar
¼ tsp salt
2 cups milk, scalded
3 slightly beaten egg yolks
2 tbsp butter
½ tsp vanilla
1 cup shredded coconut
3 egg whites
6 tbsp sugar
½ cup shredded coconut

Instructions

1. In a saucepan, mix flour, 2/3 cup sugar and salt. Gradually add scalded milk. Cook over medium heat, stirring constantly until mixture thickens and boils. Cook 2 minutes and remove from heat.
2. Add a small amount of mixture to eggs, and then combine back into the saucepan. Cook another minute, stirring constantly. Add butter, vanilla and coconut. Cool slightly.
3. Pour filling into baked pastry shell and cool completely.
4. For meringue, beat egg whites till stiff, adding 6 tbsp of sugar gradually. Spread meringue over pie filling. Sprinkle with ½ cup coconut.
5. Bake in 350-degree oven for 12-15 minutes. Cool thoroughly before serving

(After consuming, grab your pets and prepare to solve any crimes that fall into your path.)

More Books by Ellen Riggs

Bought-the-Farm Cozy Mystery Series

- *A Dog with Two Tales (prequel)*
- *Dogcatcher in the Rye*
- *Dark Side of the Moo*
- *A Streak of Bad Cluck*
- *Till the Cat Lady Sings*
- *Alpaca Lies*
- *Twas the Bite Before Christmas*
- *Swine and Punishment*
- *The Cat and the Riddle*
- *Don't Rock the Goat*
- *Swan with the Wind*
- *How to Get a Neigh with Murder*
- *Tweet Revenge*
- *For Love Or Bunny*
- *Between a Squawk and a Hard Place*
- *Double Dog Dare*
- *Deerly Departed*

Bought-the-Farm Mysteries - Boxed Sets

- *Bought the Farm Mysteries - Books 1-3*
- *Bought the Farm Mysteries - Books 4-6*

- *Bought the Farm Mysteries* - Books 7-9
- *Bought the Farm Mysteries* - Books 1-10

"Mystic Mutt Mysteries" Paranormal Cozy

- *I Want You to Haunt Me*
- *You Can't Always Get What You Haunt*
- *Any Way You Haunt It*
- *I Only Haunt to be with You*

Books by Ellen Riggs and Sandy Rideout

Dog Town Series

- *Ready or Not in Dog Town* (The Beginning)
- *Bitter and Sweet in Dog Town* (Labor Day)
- *A Match Made in Dog Town* (Thanksgiving)
- *Lost and Found in Dog Town* (Christmas)
- *Calm and Bright in Dog Town* (Christmas)
- *Tried and True in Dog Town* (New Year's)
- *Yours and Mine in Dog Town* (Valentine's Day)
- *Nine Lives in Dog Town* (Easter)
- *Great and Small in Dog Town* (Memorial Day)
- *Bold and Blue in Dog Town* (Independence Day)
- *Better or Worse in Dog Town* (Labor Day)

Dog Town Boxed Sets

- *Mischief in Dog Town* - Books 1-3
- *Mischief in Dog Town* - Books 4-7
- *Mischief in Dog Town* - Books 8-10
- *Mischief in Dog Town* - The Complete Series

Made in the USA
Monee, IL
11 September 2022